A Colonial Courtship

Cover design: Roseanna White Designs
Cover model: Abigail McGee
Model photography: Period Stock, LLC
Other images used under license from Shutterstock.com.

Library Cataloging Data
Names: McGee, Stephenia H. (Stephenia H. McGee) 1983 –
Title: A Colonial Courtship / Stephenia H. McGee
238p. 5 in. × 8 in.
Description: By The Vine Press digital eBook edition | By The Vine Press Trade paperback edition | Mississippi: By The Vine Press, 2021
Summary: Sometimes time travel is just the miracle you need. Unless it sends you to the last place you want to go.
Identifiers: LCCN: 2021931701 | ISBN-13: 978-1-63564-060-1 (trade) | 978-1-63564-059-5 (ebk.)
1. Christian Fiction 2. Time Travel Romance 3. Historical Romance 4. Clean and Wholesome Romance 5. Time Travel 6. Religious Fiction 7. Inspirational Romance

A Colonial Courtship

The Back Inn Time Series

Book Three

Stephenia H. McGee

By The Vine Press

Dear reader,

As a historical fiction writer, I've always wondered what it would be like if I could travel back in time and get a firsthand glimpse of the eras I love to read about. Thus, the idea for this series was born. It's a fun way to imagine the impossible.

Please keep in mind, dear reader, that a *story* is all this is meant to be. It is not meant to spark a theological debate on whether God would allow the miracle of time travel. The Bible tells us "Man's days are determined; You [God] have decreed the number of his months and have set limits he cannot exceed" (Job 14:5) and "My times are in your hands" (Psalm 31:15).

Several of the things regarding the time travel in this story are not possible, but it allows us to suspend what we know to be true to simply enjoy the fictional freedom of the *what if…?* So, come with me, imaginative reader, and together let's go see what it might be like to "step back *inn* time and leave our troubles behind"!

Happy reading!
Stephenia

One

Jumping off the deep end—totally losing her mind—had taken longer than expected, but it had finally happened. Abigail Martin stared up at the sweeping Victorian house and let out a sigh. Crazy. Absolutely, completely crazy. Maybe her mother really had been right about her all along.

But she was here, all the same. Chasing some story. Desperate to know the truth. Hoping for a miracle of her own.

Her friend Maddie had insisted—though she wouldn't give any details—that prayers were answered behind these walls. Something just a few months ago Abigail would have never believed.

Now, well, she had to find out for herself.

"Nice place."

The masculine voice behind her brought a cringe. She turned to look at Evan, who lifted his eyebrows skeptically. Why did he have to come? Bad enough his parents had sent *him* to pick her up from the airport.

She'd told him no less than six times she didn't need his help with her suitcase.

"Sure I can't get you to stay at my parents'?" He cast a skeptical glance at the house.

And share a room with Sarah? Both Evan and his sister would stay in their old rooms at their parents' house for the long holiday weekend. Staying with the Blakes would mean spending Thanksgiving trapped with Evan's entire family. Close quarters with people she'd avoided and a million probing questions? She couldn't think of a better way to torture herself. "Maddie highly recommended this place. Besides, staying at your house would be too weird."

Evan didn't comment. He knew what she meant. Even though they hadn't spoken in months, she had no doubt he could still read her far too easily. Which was exactly why he shouldn't be here.

Wind too chilly for Ocean Springs, Mississippi, in November tickled down the back of her neck, and she shivered. She hated the cold. "Come on."

He didn't move. "What's this really about?"

Like he didn't already know.

"This is about Atlanta, isn't it?"

And there it was. The reason she didn't want to spend the holidays with Evan's family. Even though she cared more for them than she did her own. They knew too much. They'd ask too many questions. Calling them had been a bad idea. A desperate act in a moment of weakness. No. She needed to get away.

Like, far away. Or at least try her luck at a miracle.

She glanced again at the B&B and wondered at her own gullibility. But then, obviously Maddie had gotten exactly what she'd wanted. A husband. Would this house somehow produce what Abigail longed for as well? She couldn't find out until she got rid of Evan.

Abigail shot him a scathing look. "Can we go in now? I'm freezing."

Evan shook his head, his blue eyes saying more than his lips. He felt sorry for her. Nothing like being the object of pity to make a girl feel desirable.

Not that she wanted Evan to desire her. They were friends. At least they used to be. But that was over. She marched up the wide front steps and onto the wraparound porch. Evan plodded along behind her.

She pressed the doorbell and waited.

Evan stood close to her, the enticing scent of his cologne digging up memories better forgotten. Had it really been almost ten years since she'd first laid eyes on him as a lanky high school freshman and her silly heart had gone into major crush mode?

She dared a glance at his strong jawline. Funny how being away from him for a year brought up ancient feelings. Abigail stiffened, trying to gain a hold on the way his nearness heightened her senses. Stupid. She'd conquered that ridiculous attraction a long time ago.

Friends. They'd been better off as friends.

They'd maintained their unusual friendship nearly all the way through college, with him being the popular jock and her being...well, her. They'd been close, despite their differences. At least until he'd turned his back on their friendship and—

The front door swung open, bringing Abigail's thoughts to a jarring halt. A short woman grinned at them. She wore a blue gown that made her look as if she had unnaturally wide hips with a skirt fashioned from what had to be *dozens* of yards of embroidered fabric. The square neckline was dotted with gaudy bows. Her graying curls had been piled high and topped with a little white cap.

The woman stared at Abigail as openly as Abigail stared at the woman's ornate costume. Maddie hadn't mentioned crazy outfits.

Evan chuckled, and Abigail jabbed her elbow into his ribs. The laugh cut off with a grunt.

Maddie had warned her about the quirky lady who ran this Victorian inn called The Depot, but the woman's outfit still took Abigail by surprise.

"Renaissance fair in town?" Evan asked.

The woman smiled at Evan sympathetically. "Wrong era, dear. I take it you're not familiar with history?"

Abigail couldn't help but laugh. The woman spoke sweetly, mischief dancing in her eyes.

Evan shifted his feet, appearing adequately embarrassed. Looked as if Abigail had finally found someone who could rattle that man's unshakable confidence.

"Sorry, ma'am," he said.

"Mrs. Easley." She swept a gaze over him. "And you are?"

"Evan Blake." He glanced at Abigail again, but she merely smirked. Something about this lady in period costume had him rattled.

"Mr. Blake, so that you are not caught unaware, I shall enlighten you on a bit of history." She waved for them to enter the house and closed the door on the chilly wind behind them.

Inside, the foyer of the grand house was washed in warm yellow gaslight, and the air smelled of sugar cookies. But Abigail didn't get any weird tingles. No sense of the magical.

There didn't seem to be anything special about this house aside from the intricately carved molding and fine craftsmanship. Well, that and the woman in the elaborate costume.

"This," Mrs. Easley said, gesturing down at her gown, "is not a dress from the Renaissance. It's the height of ladies' fashion from 1773."

Looking somewhat sheepish, Evan nodded. "Yes, ma'am."

Abigail smirked.

Mrs. Easley's eyes swung her way. "You must be Miss Martin. Are you familiar with the time period?"

Aside from elementary school history class? "Not particularly."

"Oh. That will present some challenges, I suppose." She waved a hand. "But no matter. Let's get you checked in, shall we? I've already looked up your room number." She eyed Evan again. "No room for this young man, though… Curious."

"He's not staying. Just helping me with my luggage."

The statement brought a smile to Mrs. Easley's lined face. "How gentlemanly." Her gaze swept over him again, assessing. "Curious indeed." She gave a dip of her chin. "I'll get your key, dear."

As soon as the woman turned her back, Evan leaned close to Abigail's ear. "That woman is seven shades of weird."

Abigail shrugged. She'd been expecting the owner to be eccentric. "She's just playing a part. Didn't you read the sign?"

"What sign?" Evan watched the woman sweep away through the doorway, her wide skirt brushing the frame on both sides.

"The one outside that talked about stepping back in time."

Evan rolled his eyes. "You pick the worst places."

She cringed at the dig. As if her confidence weren't already at an all-time low.

"Sorry." He wrapped an arm around her shoulder

and tucked her against his side. "You know I only meant this house."

"I know." He probably hadn't meant to poke her with a jab about her terrible choices. She was just too sensitive. She stepped out of his embrace.

Warm eyes watched her. Why did he have to be here? He'd shown up at the airport instead of his mother. If Abigail hadn't needed to ration what few funds she still had, she would have called an Uber in the first place. Calling Connie Blake had cost her. The conversation about why she'd refused to answer any of Evan's calls or texts was a time bomb she hoped she could continue to avoid. So far, she'd been able to turn aside Miss Connie's questions by saying she needed a little time before she was ready to answer. Women understood things like that. But then Evan had peppered her the entire ride over from the airport, and she'd used every vague answer and evasive maneuver she could think of.

Now she could see the question in his eyes again, and she was running out of excuses. She stepped toward the doorway.

"Abs, I've missed you. Tell me the truth. Why didn't you answer—?"

"She's coming back."

Mrs. Easley appeared a second later with a gigantic black key. She held it out to Abigail. "You'll be in room two." She looked at Evan again. "You plan on going all the way up with her?"

"If it's all the same to you."

Abigail withheld a groan. He'd follow her until he cornered her and forced conversations she didn't want to have. At the very least, he'd try to talk her out of staying. She didn't need him pointing out all the reasons she shouldn't take a room at the Victorian inn. Her plan was tenuous at best. If he made too many logical points about how she shouldn't spend money on a room— money she didn't have—she'd probably cave and go to his parents' house.

And she didn't want that.

"Abs, are you sure you—?"

Abigail cut him off and fired a question at Mrs. Easley. "Do you remember my friend Maddie Palmer?"

Mrs. Easley's eyes jumped from Evan to her, and a broad smile lit her face. "Of course! Are she and the captain doing well?"

"Happily married."

She clasped her hands, clearly delighted. "Oh, how wonderful. I love how everything works out according to His plan."

Evan relaxed next to her. A subtle easing of his shoulders. A slight release of breath. Things she only noticed because she knew him so well. Had the woman's reference to God set him at ease? Interesting. Regardless, maybe now he wouldn't pester her about staying here.

Mrs. Easley gestured up the stairs, and Abigail gripped the key. Before the woman could turn away she said, "This might sound weird, but I'm curious. Did anything"—she glanced at Evan—"unusual happen to Maddie and Nate while they were here?"

The woman lifted her eyebrows. "What do you classify as unusual?"

Abigail had a suspicion. Something that Maddie had hinted at but hadn't said outright. Something totally and completely impossible.

Time travel.

The suspicion had brought Abigail here. The ridiculous hope that she could find a way to go back and undo what she'd done in Atlanta. Or at the very least, go to the beginning of her family's problems and see the truth for herself.

Evan tensed beside her again, and she could feel his eyes boring into her. Almost as though he thought he could dig into her brain and find answers there.

Stupid. Why hadn't she waited until Evan was gone to ask? Her and her wayward mouth. When would she ever learn to *think* before talking? Saying bizarre things out loud, especially in front of Evan, would lead to him dragging her out of here and straight to his sister. And she did *not* need a forced session with a shrink. Regardless of what people kept saying, she wasn't crazy.

Abigail laughed it off. "You know, magical moments to fall in love."

A slow smile curved Mrs. Easley's lips. "Is that what you came here for?"

Uh-oh. This was going downhill in a hurry. Laughing again, though it sounded painfully forced, Abigail waved a hand as though she could shoo away the awkwardness. "Nope. Just want to get away. Do something new."

Mrs. Easley smirked. "Leaving troubles behind and finding something new is our specialty."

She felt, rather than saw, Evan roll his eyes. "Offer still stands, Abs."

Before she could think better of what was probably another terrible choice, Abigail marched up the stairs. After three steps, Evan scrambled after her.

"She'll need your help, son," Mrs. Easley called after them. "Do try to keep an open mind."

"That woman is wacko," Evan grumbled as soon as they reached the top of the stairs. "You need to get out of here."

"I'm staying." Now if for no other reason than the fact that he was telling her not to.

"Then I will too."

"That's stupid."

He planted his feet in the middle of the hallway. "What's gotten into you? Not only have you refused to talk to me since you left for Atlanta, but now you're acting like I'm your enemy." Pain flicked in his eyes. "Can we talk?"

"I just need a little space. Time to think things through."

Evan watched her a second, then stepped closer. "More time than all those months in Atlanta?" She refused to answer, but he kept watching her anyway as though he could read her thoughts on her face. After a moment, he sighed. "You seem to be searching for something."

And there he was decoding her again. She reached for the familiar comfort of sarcasm. "I'm looking for a place to spend my time off where people won't pepper me with a million questions."

Not even a cringe. "I'm here for you. You know that, right?"

She offered a tight smile. "I'm in room two. Must be down the hall." She whirled around and scurried away.

"Interesting paintings," Evan said behind her.

The out-of-place statement caught her off guard. She paused. "What?"

Evan gestured to a frame hanging on the wall in front of him. "Woman must be obsessed with the Revolutionary period."

He was baiting her. Trying to keep her talking. "Room's this way." If he wasn't going to follow, she'd grab her suitcase out of the hall later.

"Huh."

Now what? She turned again. Evan was leaning

close to the picture, squinting. "That man looks like me."

"Just leave the suitcase. I'll get it."

"I'm serious." He reached out and touched the painting but suddenly jerked back as though something had bitten him.

Evan stumbled and grabbed at his chest.

Abigail screamed. She reached him just as he crumpled to the floor. "Help! Someone help." She dropped to her knees beside him, grabbing his face in her hands.

Heat suddenly poured through her. Her head swam.

Dizzy. Why was she so dizzy?

Should have never—

Everything went black.

Two

This had to be the worst headache of his life.

Evan massaged his temples and drew long breaths. He hadn't felt this mowed over since an Alabama left tackle ear-holed him his senior year at Mississippi State.

Slowly, the pain receded, allowing his thoughts to focus on something other than the throbbing. He quickly assessed his position. Lying on his back, softness beneath him.

Not the floor.

He tried to think back.

He'd been in the hallway. Everything had started to go dark. He vaguely remembered hitting the floor, followed by Abigail's frantic shout.

He'd blacked out.

Another thought occurred, pulling him further out of the murky area between sleep and wakefulness. Had he been carried to the hospital? Abigail would be worried. And he'd need to call his parents. Let them know, if she hadn't already.

He forced his eyes open. Above him, a wood beam ceiling supported pale white walls. Definitely not a hospital. He blinked at the ceiling until his eyes regained clear sight. Slowly, his gaze drifted around the room. All the furniture looked antique. He groaned and sat up. He must be in Abigail's bed at the weird hotel where she wanted to spend Thanksgiving.

Instead of with him.

He swung his feet off the lumpy bed and dropped them to a woven rug on the floor. He paused. His lower calves were covered with stockings, and his feet had been shoved into goofy shoes with pointy toes and low heels. Knee-length pants similar to ones he'd worn in football wrapped his thighs. Heat bubbled up in his middle.

Had that crazy woman dressed him in one of her wacko costumes while he'd been passed out? He gripped his head, still trying to get the fog in his brain to clear.

What had happened?

He'd seen a painting in the hall depicting a harbor with historical ships, the kind with three tall masts and sails. Men had been pictured shouting on the docks, holding lanterns and wearing triangular hats. One of those men had been pointing at the ships. That guy had looked a lot like him. He'd reached out and touched the painting.

Then—nothing. Why had he passed out? He shook his head and pushed off the mattress, his mind clearing.

Across from the bed, a floor-length mirror with wavy glass offered a hazy reflection.

What on God's green earth? Evan ground his teeth. He wore a pair of brown, way-too-tight pants, women's white stockings, a white shirt he could only describe as frilly with all that lacy stuff around his neck and wrists, and a gray vest with a bunch of metal buttons.

Too far, lady. Way too far.

He'd give that Mrs. Easley a piece of his mind. What kind of person undressed another while he was sleeping? Not one he wanted around Abigail. He stalked across the room, barely noticing the lengths the woman had gone to for her B&B's theme.

He needed to find Abigail and get them out of there. ASAP. She'd protest, but this time he'd speak his mind. There was absolutely no reason she needed to stay with a creepy old woman at a weird hotel when she would be much more comfortable at his parents' house.

They were like family. Or had been, once.

He'd promised himself the moment Abigail Martin had waltzed back into his life that he'd take a four-hundred-pound linebacker stomping his face before he'd lose her again. He wasn't the coward he'd been in high school. Or the prideful jerk he'd been in college. God and knee injuries had a way of humbling a man. And giving him perspective.

This time, Evan wouldn't let Abigail face trouble alone. This time, he'd be there for her. And maybe even tell her how he felt.

When the time was right.

First, he had to get her out of this creepy house. He jerked open the door and stalked into the hallway.

And froze.

This wasn't the hallway he remembered. Lined with dark wood paneling and dripping candles on wall sconces, this wasn't the airy B&B with its floral wallpaper and lace-lined windows. No series of paintings from different time periods hung on the walls.

Unease clawed in his stomach. Maybe he was just in a different part of the house. "Abigail?"

He walked slowly, nerves tingling. A door down the hall stood open. He moved that direction, adrenaline heightening his senses. "Abigail?"

Someone groaned. He paused, listening. The sound came from the room with the open door. He sprinted the remaining distance and launched himself through the doorway. "Abigail!"

She lay crumpled on the floor, clothed in mounds of a shimmering brownish-gold fabric. He dropped to her side and gripped her shoulder. Long lashes fluttered against her flushed cheeks, then opened to reveal the most beautiful bluish-green hazel eyes he'd ever seen.

Blinking, she seemed to have trouble focusing. Did her head hurt? He eased his fingers into her thick mahogany hair, which had been curled and pinned to her head, looking for signs of injury. Something he hadn't even considered for himself. The up-do made feeling around on her scalp difficult, but he didn't think there was anything—

"Evan?" Her voice pinched with concern. "Are you okay?"

Was *he* okay? "I'm fine." He didn't feel any lumps on her head. He leaned close. "What happened?"

"I don't know." She blinked again. "My brain feels foggy."

"Mine did too. It's better now." He sat back. If that woman had drugged them, they had much bigger problems than her dressing them up like dolls. The idea made his skin crawl.

Abigail drew in a long breath and let it out slowly. She closed her eyes, and when she opened them again, they seemed clearer. Those two-toned depths reeled him in.

She suddenly sat up, forcing him to move back. Her gaze darted around the small room, which was packed with more antique furniture. "Where are we?"

"In that stupid hotel." Probably in a different part. He hoped. But maybe not. He had no idea where they were. Not that he would freak her out by saying so.

"Why are you wearing that outfit?" Her face twisted into a scowl. "It's not nice to make fun of the hostess woman."

Hostess woman? "You mean the B&B owner? I'm guessing she's the one who put me in this getup."

Abigail patted the dress mounded up around her legs as though noticing it for the first time. "You mean she dressed us in costumes while we were passed out?"

The fear in her voice sent tingles through him. He wrapped a protective arm around her shoulders. "I'm getting you out of here."

She nodded weakly. He had to help her to her feet. Yards of fabric trimmed in tons of lace pooled around her, tangling her legs and causing her to grunt as she fought against the constraint.

"Should have known better," she grumbled.

Evan kept a firm grip on Abigail's elbow. "About what?"

She cut a sharp glance at him as though she hadn't expected him to hear her. "It doesn't matter." She drew in a determined breath and straightened her spine in that way she did when she wanted the world to witness her defiance. They stepped into the hallway, and she paused. "This isn't the same hall." She glanced around. "And where is my suitcase?"

"I'll come back for it." Probably with a few policemen in tow.

He pulled her to a set of stairs. Noise drifted up from the lower floor he hadn't noticed before. Some kind of party? Wrapping an arm around Abigail's waist, he guided her down the stairs.

Smells assaulted him. Meat, primarily. But also fermented scents of alcohol and…livestock? What kind of place did this woman run?

They descended into another hallway, and a thin woman wearing a stained apron bustled out of a swinging door, her hands laden with a massive tray topped with heaping plates. She cast a quick glance at them and bobbed her head.

Another woman, younger than the first but also garbed in a historical costume, hurried out of the door and through another across the hall. No one seemed interested in stopping Abigail and him. He led her down the dim hallway and toward a door at the far end. One that hopefully led them out of the *Twilight Zone*.

Bristling with the tingle of nervous energy, Evan half-dragged Abigail past what looked to be a busy kitchen and through the heavy wood door with a metal doorknob.

He drew up short as soon as they stepped outside.

"A barn?" Abigail turned slowly, the hem of her dress grazing the dirt. "There wasn't a barn."

They'd exited the building—which was absolutely not the pretentious Victorian with wraparound porches—and stepped outside into a stable yard. Carriages were parked in a line, and men dressed in clothes similar to his own tugged horses on leather reins in and out of the wooden barn.

The overwhelming smell of horses had him wanting

to put a hand over his nose. He cleared his throat. "Looks like she moved us."

Abigail gaped at him.

At six-four and two hundred and thirty pounds, Evan wasn't an easy man to move. The psycho woman must have had help.

The look on Abigail's face said she'd thought the same. Glistening eyes drilled into him. "Where *are* we?"

His muscles tensed. "Doesn't matter. We're getting out of here."

Abigail clung to his arm, and he headed across the muddy stable area, past the barn teeming with horses, and through a gate onto a street.

One filled with more people dressed in costumes. Costumes ranging from ridiculously elaborate to dirty and simple. Several men walked by in bright red coats trimmed in white. Some men worn tight pants and frilly shirts with long-tailed jackets. Every woman wore a dress. From the fancy type like Abigail had on to humble dark fabrics brushing around their ankles.

Every outfit seemed disturbingly authentic. Not that he could tell for sure. He'd never been the type to frequent Renaissance fairs or historical reenactments.

Through the jumble of smells assaulting him, he caught a whiff of the salty sea air.

"Come on." He tugged Abigail from where she stood gaping at the people and animals around them. "We'll get out of this festival and to a regular street.

Then we can get a cab or Uber or something."

Too bad Mrs. Easley had stolen his cell along with his clothes. As soon as he got to a phone, that lady was going to jail.

Abigail clung to him, for once not arguing with his plan. Her nails dug into his arm.

He rubbed his fingers over hers and steered her around a particularly muddy patch of the cobbled street. A team of horses clomped their direction, and he quickened his pace. "It'll be okay. Once we get out of here, we'll report her."

"Not at all what Maddie said," Abigail mumbled.

"What?"

She shook her head, lips sealed. He'd ask later. Right now, the ordeal probably had her in some kind of shock. He felt close to cracking himself.

They scurried to the other side of the road. A man in a red coat with rows of metal buttons and a pair of white pants marched toward them. Each shoulder of his jacket had golden tassels, and he looked like he had dressed as a British soldier from a colonial movie. Evan raised a hand. "Excuse me. Could I borrow your phone?"

The man raked an assessing gaze over them. Eyes narrowed, he didn't even bother to acknowledge Evan before continuing past them.

Go figure. Acting as though they didn't know about anything modern. Stupid. Why did people want to pretend they lived in the past? Weren't they glad for things like electricity and cell phones?

Grumbling about rude weirdos under his breath, Evan guided Abigail through the horde of people darting around them. Whatever reenactment scenario these people portrayed, they did so with gusto. The sights, sounds, and smells that pommeled him were nearly overwhelming.

If not for the need to keep Abigail safe and provide her with a calming presence, he'd probably scream. Horses neighed, men shouted, and dirty children scuttled through the throng.

Where were their parents?

Finally, he and Abigail turned down another street and out of the teeming mass. Ahead, pristine blue sky met a glistening ocean.

Filled with ships.

Tall, three-masted ships.

All other thoughts fled his brain, and Evan stumbled to a halt. There were no ships like that in the Gulf of Mexico.

Mouth dry, he clung to Abigail as they stared out over the unimaginable sight before them.

Impossible. Abigail's heart pounded in her chest. She'd

suspected…well, sort of wondered about the time travel. No one could have expected *this*. Maddie had said a few weird things about going out on old-fashioned dates with Nate. Strange things about her young grandparents. But when Abigail had prodded for more, Maddie'd been vague.

This must be why.

Had Maddie met Nate in the past? Brought him back to the future? Was that why she'd never seen the guy before Maddie up and announced she was getting married?

Whoa.

Talk about a miracle. Maddie had gone back to somewhere in the past and snagged herself a man. Brought him home like a prized marlin on a deep sea excursion.

Abigail's mind raced with the possibilities. If only she could think straight with the wind constantly nipping at her.

An icy breeze cut across the back of her neck, and she shivered. Even wrapped in all this fabric, the cold seeped into her. She hated the cold. Why couldn't they have time-traveled to somewhere warmer?

Deep inside, she sensed she really should be more upset about the current situation, but all she felt was a sense of awe…and the unnerving cold. If time travel was possible, then she could find out the truth. The *real* truth about what her father had done. Maybe even undo some of her own choices. Like ever going to Atlanta in the first place.

If *this* was possible, anything was possible. Maddie had been right. A miracle. But shouldn't the time warp have also taken her to her heart's deepest desire as it had for Maddie?

Must be some kind of glitch. Because the middle of a frozen street staring at ancient ships was just about the farthest thing possible from Abigail's heart's desire.

Beside her, Evan stood like a bear on the verge of attack. Uh-oh. Abigail forced herself to focus and rein in her galloping thoughts. Evan wasn't supposed to be a part of this. The shock probably got the best of him. He'd never been the type with an active imagination, and time travel landed way outside of his in-the-box kind of thinking. She'd better get him under control before he went berserk. She threaded her fingers through his, hoping to infuse a little of her unnatural calm into his tense hand.

He drew a sharp breath as though he'd forgotten she stood by him and looked down at her from his towering height. Even at five-eight, she could still wear heels next to Evan. In her current weird little low-heeled boots, however, she had tilt her head back. "It's okay." She squeezed his hand and spoke soothingly. "We're okay."

"Okay?" Evan threw a hand out toward the harbor like a Hail Mary pass. "Are you seeing this?"

So much for soothing. She looked at the ships again. The sight of the harbor only brought confirmation of what her instincts already knew. "We went back to the past."

Evan whirled to face her. "Are you out of your mind?"

She glared at him. "No."

He gripped the back of his neck, voice lowering. "Time travel is impossible, Abs."

"So are ships in the harbor straight out of a history book. And all the people dressed in costumes." She gestured to his clothes. "*And* so is waking up in—"

"I get it." The muscle in the side of his square jaw ticked. "But this doesn't make any sense."

"Maddie said miracles happened at The Depot."

Evan watched her until she met his gaze. "Come again?"

She infused strength into her posture. "Clearly we aren't in Ocean Springs anymore, Dorothy."

His dark eyebrows drew low over his nose.

So much for her joke. "You have a better explanation?"

"Yeah." He practically barked the word. "That woman drugged us, dressed us up like dolls, and moved us to the middle of a history reenactment."

Abigail stared at the massive ships. Men moved up and down gangplanks, unloading crates and shouting to one another. "Most elaborate reenactment I've ever seen."

Evan's gaze followed hers. "Can't explain those. Unless we've been moved to a different city."

"Or state."

That had him clenching his jaw again. How would Mrs. Easley have transferred them to a different state? More importantly, why?

Evan grabbed her hand again. "Come on. Someone has to have a phone we can use."

"A phone? I'm guessing this is 1773."

He stopped again. "Why?"

"That was the year she mentioned. The clothes she wore came from that year, as I'm guessing ours do as well."

Evan rubbed his forehead. "People can't send people back to the past."

Abigail shrugged. "We got here somehow." Biting wind stung her eyes. "How about we go back to…wherever we woke up? Look for clues."

"We need to find someone not taking part in the reenactment. These people like to pretend the modern world doesn't exist."

He still thought they were in an excessively elaborate production? That all these people were actors? Granted, people could be convincing when they wanted to portray a different life, but this many? Seemed unlikely.

"Can we at least get out of the cold? If this is just a reenactment, then we aren't in any danger, right?"

His eyes flicked around their surroundings. She could practically see the wheels turning behind those startling blue eyes. "Fine. We regroup. Demand someone give us a phone."

"Or find ours in our rooms."

Evan's eyebrows shot up. "You think that woman stashed our stuff there?"

No. But then, Abigail also thought they were in 1773. "Does it hurt to look?" A shiver overtook her. "Please? I don't like standing out here on the street."

Apparently, that was the key to getting her large companion to move. Maybe he was also suffering from the icy air that was making her nose run. He wrapped a protective arm around her, and she relished the warmth of his body.

"Let's get you settled. I'll figure this out."

Abigail remained silent as he guided her away from the docks and steered them back the way they'd come. At the intersection, they turned onto the busy street they'd discovered after passing through the stables.

Evan flagged down the first man they came to. "Excuse me, sir. I know this breaks your fantasy rules, but we have an emergency. Can I please use your phone?"

The short man's thin face scrunched. "I beg your pardon?"

Interesting accent. British-sounding, but not like what she'd heard in movies.

Evan sighed. "Please, drop the act for just a second. We were abducted and need to make a call."

The man drew back. "Abducted, you say?"

Oh boy. This could go bad in a hurry. But then, who was she to say they hadn't been abducted? If nothing else, talking to this man could prove—or disprove—her time-travel theory.

The man pointed a long finger down the road. "There's a constable's office ahead, should you need to report a crime."

Evan groaned.

Abigail cut him off before he could come unglued. "Thank you, kind sir."

The man shifted suspicious eyes from Evan to her and bobbed his head. "Good day to you." He scurried off before Evan could say anything more.

"At least there's some kind of police." He tugged on her arm. "Let's go."

What happened to going back to their rooms?

Abigail allowed Evan to pull her along. One way or another one of them would be proved right. If he didn't believe her, maybe he'd believe the people they encountered.

They passed the building they'd woken up in. Some kind of tavern. At least it had been warm in there. She assessed each building they passed. Not a hint of the modern era. No power lines. No paved streets. No stoplights or even red octagonal stop signs. People in costume was one thing. An entire town was another.

How could Evan not realize they'd stepped into the past? Colonial, obviously. But where? Boats put them on the coast, and the cold insisting on seeping into her clothing and the bits of icy snow clinging to doorframes indicated New England.

She groaned as Evan tugged her past people who seemed oblivious to the biting wind. Shouldn't she and Evan also be dressed in long woolen cloaks or something like the rest of these people?

"Anyone got a phone?" Evan suddenly called. His voice carried over the heads of the people around them, all shorter than Abigail. Even the men. Evan's height appeared massive. "Anyone willing to drop the act for fifty bucks and a chance to stop a criminal?"

People paused now, looking at him warily. No shifting glances at one another at the mention of money. No hands reaching for hidden pockets. These people didn't have a clue what he was talking about.

"Evan." Abigail yanked his arm until he looked down at her. "Stop. Please."

He opened his mouth, then closed it and frowned. "Trust me. Something's not right about these people. Fifty should've had someone reaching for a phone."

The onlookers began walking away again, dismissing the outburst, though they gave Abigail and Evan a wide berth.

Evan grunted. "Come on. We'll have to go to the

police. At least they'll be obligated to drop the act."

"I don't think it's an act." His eyes darkened, and she hurried on. "Please. For me. Can we go back to that tavern and look in the rooms we woke up in?"

A flash of fear crossed his face. Was he afraid of being taken advantage of again?

Abigail hurried on. "We won't let anyone near us. She won't take us by surprise."

Evan glanced back down the street, toward what she assumed would be the constable's office.

"Or I suppose you could go on to the law, and I'll head back up to the room." She snatched her arm from him and turned, shuffling away in her big skirt before he could react.

A second later he had her arm again. "You can't go back there alone."

She withheld a grin. "Then I guess you'll have to come with me."

And just like that, she remembered how satisfying it felt to outmaneuver Evan Blake.

Grumbling, he gave a small shake of his head and gestured for her to lead the way.

Three

Abigail had lost her mind. Evan watched her closely as they walked down the same street again. Sarah would say something about people pretending to have outward calm whenever they were hiding overwhelming internal emotions. Though his sister would also use a bunch of technical terms or some other brain-melting string of words he couldn't decipher. She'd always had a way of doing that. Making him feel dumb. Or scrutinized.

Realization hit him. That was it. *That* was why Abigail hadn't wanted to stay with his family. The thought lightened his step. She wasn't trying to get away from *him*. She simply didn't want to be analyzed by his sister.

Except from the looks of it, maybe she did need to talk to someone. And Sarah was good at her job. Something had happened to Abigail that had made her leave everyone she knew behind. Had made her refuse to speak to him. Then, more recently, had her calling his mother in tears and returning to Ocean Springs.

The woman who'd come back from Atlanta wasn't the friend he remembered. And the woman currently stalking down the street in the middle of a highly stressful situation wasn't the fun-loving girl he'd known since he was a kid.

Did she really believe in time travel?

Despite all the oddities around them, there had to be a logical explanation.

God, we could use a little help here. Please show Abigail we haven't bent time and space. Please prove to her that wormholes aren't among Your miracles.

He held the door open to the bustling building they'd woken up in. The reenactors had certainly chosen a well-preserved historical site.

And please help her find whatever it is she's looking for. Show me how to help her.

Women still moved between the kitchen and the dining area. His stomach grumbled. What time of day was it anyway? He had been so overwhelmed that he hadn't paid attention. It felt later than midday but too early for supper.

They took the staircase and returned to the upper hallway. The door to the room he'd occupied stood open. He quickly took stock of the furnishings. Full-sized bed with a lumpy mattress. Small writing table. Boxy looking wardrobe.

He strode to the wardrobe first and pulled it open. Inside, costumes hung on wooden hangers and pegs.

Abigail looked around him as he rifled through the clothing.

"Nothing. My clothes, and I'm guessing my phone and wallet, are missing." He sighed. "Can we go to the police now?"

Her eyes roamed his face a second, and then she pushed past him and grabbed one of the costumes. She held a long-tailed jacket in front of him. "Your size, I'd guess."

"So?"

"So, looks like someone went through an awful lot of trouble to stick you in the middle of some kind of production, don't you think?"

Clothing that might fit him didn't prove anything. He searched the writing desk, finding nothing more than little pots of ink and fancy-looking feather pens. Authentic to the smallest detail. No one went through that much trouble except—

He whirled around to face Abigail. "I know where we are!"

Surprise lifted her features. "You do?"

"Of course. It's Williamsburg. I'd forgotten all about this place, but I remember hearing about a town in Virginia where they hire actors, and tourists come to watch reenactments of Revolutionary battles." He took a quick breath, excitement at having solved the mystery of their location making his words come faster. "The entire town is built to be completely authentic. That's why there're no power lines. No people with cell phones. Their job is to pretend they live in the 1700s." He rocked back on his heels, pleased he'd figured out the truth.

Abigail thought a moment, then gave a small nod. Relief swept through him.

"But how did we get to Williamsburg? That's bound to be at least a twelve-hour drive, if not more."

"She must have kept us drugged."

Another small nod. "And people come to this place to see what life was like in the colonies?"

"Yeah," he said, drawing out the word. What was she getting at?

"So where are all the tourists?"

His pulse ratcheted. "Must be rehearsal day or something."

"Must be." She didn't sound convinced. Abigail offered him a tight smile and then scurried out of the room.

Fine. Maybe he was missing something here, but what happened to trusting your friends enough to give them the benefit of the doubt?

Evan groaned and followed her. "Where are you going?"

"To my room to look for our phones. Remember?"

He caught up to her in three strides. The door to the room he'd found her in also stood open. Decorated much the same as his, the small space held a bed, desk, and wardrobe. Abigail marched to the wardrobe, flung open the door, and then gestured to the interior with a Vanna White flourish.

Colorful fabric overflowed from inside. He caught her eye. "And?"

"More clothes in my size, of course. Don't you see? All this is here for us."

"For what purpose?" This was insane. "You're telling me we got sent back in time and have assigned rooms complete with clothes that fit us?"

She nodded.

Frustration clenched his stomach. "You don't think, just for a moment, that we were knocked out, dressed in crazy costumes, and stashed in rooms containing more costumes for, oh I don't know, one of the dozens of people who work here?"

Doubt flickered on her face.

He pushed further. "Isn't it possible we are victims of a criminal obsessed with the past who decided to teach me a lesson for making light of her passion?"

Abigail crossed her arms over her stiff-looking dress, doubt further pulling down the corners of her full mouth. "But Maddie is happy." The words were grumbled under her breath, and he barely caught them.

"What?"

Abigail suddenly threw up her hands. "Maddie. My friend. She went to The Depot. Came back madly in love, got married, and all her dreams came true. At her party in October, she told me that The Depot was special. That wishes came true there. Miracles. I wanted to find out for myself. I get it now. Maddie wasn't saying it was *like* she'd gone back in time. She actually did."

His thoughts snagged on only one part of her tirade. "You came home in October?"

Abigail gave him a look that said he'd missed the most important part of her statement. Fine. They'd return to that later.

He focused on the rest of the crazy things she'd said and tried to untangle the rush of words. "Let me make sure I understand. Your friend told you she went to a B&B and it sent her back in time, so you decided you were going to see if you could time-travel too?"

She twisted her fingers together. "It's not as crazy as it sounds."

It wasn't? He opened his mouth, then snapped his teeth closed hard enough to jar them. The way she was looking at him said he'd better tread carefully. Forcing himself to release some of the tension from his shoulders, he took out the small chair at the writing desk, spun it around, and sat.

Abigail had a friend who'd found love. Gotten married. Obviously the miracle this friend had experienced was meeting a man ready for commitment. Was that what Abigail was really looking for?

The idea sent heat up his sternum, and he rubbed at

the lace gathered at his neck. Why did people dress in such itchy clothes? He crossed his ankle over his knee and took a good look at the woman across from him.

She stood tall, watching him with keen eyes that said she was waiting for him to cut her down in some way and, as soon as he did, she'd be ready to pounce.

Patience.

The word impressed itself on his brain the way things sometimes did when he felt God move in his spirit. Rather than refute her, he tried for understanding.

"What time did she visit?"

The question seemed to deflate some of Abigail's hostility. She wrinkled her nose in that cute little way he adored. "I don't know. She didn't say."

Oh boy. "You said she experienced a miracle. What do you think that miracle was?"

Something flicked in her eyes, and her expression turned guarded again. "Time travel."

She was pretty stuck on the time travel thing. "Okay." Her perception was her reality. Until he could prove the truth to her, he wouldn't stir an argument.

"Really?" She instantly relaxed, turning from sandpaper to cotton in one release of breath. "You believe me?"

He didn't want to lie, but the temptation to have her keep looking at him as if he'd just rescued her from a mustached villain who'd tied her up on the train tracks needled him. He cleared his throat. "I believe your friend experienced something special, and you were looking to find something special yourself."

Her gaze lowered.

"Am I right?"

"Yes. But that doesn't mean it isn't possible." Flashing eyes met his. "Look around you."

This argument was going in circles. And the longer they sat here debating the impossible, the longer a criminal got away with her crimes. Evan rose. "Let's talk about this later. Can we at least agree we need to get home?"

She hesitated.

Alarm spiked through him. "You don't want to go home?"

"Of course I do." She looked away again. "Just…maybe not yet."

Abigail believed they had traveled back in time, and she didn't want to go home. Why? Because she believed her friend Maddie had found love in the past?

Suddenly, he had a whole lot less time to tell her the truth about his feelings than he'd imagined.

How could she make him understand? But then, Abigail didn't really understand what was happening either. Somewhere in her gut, she knew they'd time-traveled.

The why-here-and-now part, well, that still evaded her. And though she didn't want to admit it, even to herself, she was glad Evan had been sucked into the madness with her.

Finding herself in the past might have been much scarier if she didn't have his comforting presence. Even if he did currently look like a bear in colonial clothing. All tense and aggravated and completely out of place.

Of all the times she'd imagined facing Evan again, this scenario never made the list.

"You're right. We need to figure out how to get home. Regardless of where—or when—we are." She plucked at the lace hanging from her elbow. "But first I want to know how we got here."

"Something we can agree on." He rose and gestured to the door. "To the police?"

She'd hoped they would find evidence in their rooms that would explain what had happened. Or at least prove she was right. But they were no closer to the truth than they had been when they'd first arrived. She needed to think, but her thoughts felt jumbled.

"Hello?" A feminine voice called from the hallway. A middle-aged woman appeared a second later. Her eyes widened as her glance darted between the two of them, but quickly smoothed.

"Hi," Abigail said, sharing a glance with Evan.

She inclined her head in acknowledgement, then focused on Evan. "Mr. Warren wants to know if you'll be stabling any horses with us. And…" she glanced around and lowered her voice. "He said to let you know the meeting will go on as scheduled."

"Meeting?"

The woman shifted uncomfortably. "You're a mason, right?"

Masons. Meetings. Ships in the harbor. The pieces of the puzzle fired themselves at her, and excitement bubbled in Abigail's chest. "The Sons of Liberty," she blurted.

The woman darted a glance at Abigail, and a small smile played at her lips. She turned back to look at Evan, and as soon as her back was to Abigail, Abigail nodded vigorously at Evan. *Play along*, she mouthed.

He frowned.

Please, she mouthed again. *For me?*

Evan's face twisted in a scowl, but he nodded at the woman.

"May I ask your recommendation for a dressmaker here in *Boston*?" Abigail asked before Evan could say anything that might make this woman realize he wasn't a mason or a visiting patriot here to help plan what, if she guessed correctly, would be the upcoming Boston Tea Party.

The woman smiled, not seeming bothered by the change in subject. "Certainly, Miss. Many of the ladies prefer Mrs. Westerfield's shop. Shall I send for a carriage?"

Aha! She was right. The woman hadn't corrected her. They *were* in Boston. Abigail grinned at Evan. "No, thank you. Mr. Blake will escort me once his business is complete, I'm sure."

"Of course, miss. Send for me if you require anything further. Good day to you both."

Once she was out of the room, Abigail flashed Evan a smile of triumph. "Boston, 1773. I was right."

He stared at her. "Not possible."

Maybe not. But then again, here they were. Why here, and why now? And how in the world was she going to figure out how to make this time machine work in her favor? Seventeen seventy-three was more than two centuries too early. How did one control the *where* of the time travel? She had to figure out how to point this contraption where she wanted to go.

Evan put his head in his hands, the sag in his wide shoulders drawing her attention. "This is going to be the worst Thanksgiving ever."

Four

ime for this masquerade to end. Evan marched into the squatty building he assumed belonged to the security for this little play-acting town and inside a dim office that relied only on the murky light pouring through leaded glass windows.

Abigail followed and closed the heavy wooden door.

A man rose from a large desk that looked as though it belonged in the quarters of a wealthy captain on one of those giant ships in the harbor.

The man wore another of the ridiculous costumes, with his hair long, curly, and held back in a ponytail at the base of his neck. He appeared to be in his early thirties.

"How may I help you?" the man asked, his gaze sweeping over Evan.

No computers. No monitors. No phone on the desk. Did the charade extend this far? No, there had to be a room in the back where they'd hidden the modern equipment.

"Look, I know it's your job to keep up the act for the tourists, but my friend and I have an emergency and we need to make calls to—"

"You wish to report a crime?" The man's eyebrows plunged toward his nose as he held up a hand.

"A woman abducted us, dressed us in costumes, and stole our belongings."

Abigail shifted next to him but thankfully remained quiet. He didn't need her spouting crazy notions like time travel.

The man stared at him a moment. "Abducted?"

Did this man need hearing aids? "Yes. She dressed us in costumes and robbed us." He gestured down the front of his outfit. "We don't work here. And we aren't tourists."

The man stared at him. "A woman?" He sounded incredulous. "What woman?"

Finally they were getting somewhere. "Mrs. Easley. I don't know how she got us here but—"

"I'm not familiar with the Easley family."

Who cared if he knew the family? "We just want to get out of here. We can file a report later."

Again the man seemed confused. "Did you not come here to make a report?"

He opened his mouth, frustration tightening his throat. If this man wasn't going to help—

"Sir," Abigail stepped forward. "If I may?"

He gave a nod.

"My name is Miss Abigail Martin, and this is my companion Mr. Evan Blake."

What was with all the mister-and-miss stuff?

The man gave a slight bow. "Francis Barnard."

Oh boy. Talk about overboard. These people were out of their ever-loving minds.

"Forgive us for being a bit disoriented, Mr. Barnard," Abigail continued, speaking as though she were giving a monologue in a play. "We do not know how we came to be in the city. As I'm sure you can imagine, such circumstances might leave a person befuddled."

Evan stared at her. Where in the world did she learn to talk like that? And why was she pandering to their stupid games? But then, maybe he should give her the benefit of the doubt. Maybe she thought she could play along and get the man to cooperate.

The man seemed to relax. "Certainly, Miss. How may I assist you?"

Looked like Abigail's play might outsmart the defense after all.

"First, if you would be so kind, would you please tell me exactly where we are and what might be today's date?"

The side of his mouth twitched. "It is the thirteenth of December in the year of our Lord 1773."

Evan rolled his eyes. Francis didn't notice.

"We are on Union Street in Boston, Massachusetts Colony."

This wasn't news to anyone. Of course the man would spout off his rehearsed lines about their location. A tingle raced across his skin, making him feel itchy. Hadn't Abigail guessed they were in Boston earlier? Had she seen a pamphlet or something? Unease tightened his chest.

"And the establishment down the road," Abigail continued. "The one with a dragon over the door?"

"The Green Dragon, Miss." He tugged on his lapels. "Are you reporting misconduct at the Dragon?"

She shook her head. "No, sir. I don't believe so. Merely that my companion and I do not know how we came to be at the establishment."

Francis huffed. "Sounds like an issue to take up with Mr. Warren."

"And he is?"

"Owner of the tavern."

This was going nowhere. Evan squared his shoulders. He had nearly a good foot in height on the man. Stepping closer, he caused the guy to have to look up at him. He'd grown past using intimidating others to get his way, but this could be an exception. He hardened his voice. "Can we please stop pretending now? We need to use a phone. Catch a flight or an Uber or whatever home. Then you can bet I'll be filing charges against this tourist trap for obstruction of justice."

Both Abigail and Francis stared at him. Her lips pulled downward, showing her disappointment. He couldn't help that right now. He shifted his focus to Francis only to find a mixture of confusion and wariness on his face. Such a statement should have had the guy dropping his act. The fact that it didn't meant either this man was a better actor than Evan imagined, or...well, he didn't want to think about the alternative.

Please, God. End this. Show the truth.

Francis shot a concerned look to Abigail. "Disoriented, you say?" He placed a hand on his desk and narrowed his eyes at Evan. "Should we relieve you of the company of this man until he regains his wits?"

Regain his wits? Of all the—

Abigail gripped Evan's arm. "No, sir. That's not necessary. I believe he will see the truth shortly."

Truth his foot. Desperation clawed up his throat. No. It just wasn't possible. "Fine. I won't press charges. Please, just let us use a phone."

"Phone?" The man blinked at him.

Abigail tugged on his arm. "Let's go."

Evan planted his feet.

"Please, before they lock you up for being crazy. They do that." Her voice lowered. "And I'm afraid to be here alone."

Snapping out of the anger that had started to narrow his vision, Evan tucked Abigail's hand into his and stalked out the door. Outside, horses, carts and carriages clogged the street. Every detail perfect. Every person in character.

But it couldn't be real. Couldn't be.

"Don't you see?" Abigail tugged against him. "We *are* in the past." Her voice held far too much excitement.

"Not possible," he grunted. Weren't any of his suggestions for logical alternatives worth considering? She could at least try to see things his way, even if he was struggling to find evidence of the truth.

"I say we go back to the tavern where we woke up. I remember enough from my American History class to have an idea what's going on. We're staying at the Green Dragon. It's famous for being a secret meeting place for patriots. Don't you want to see what it was really like?"

"Why?" Evan practically barked the word. "Why do you care? Why do you want to be here? Is my family that bad that you'd rather stay…" He gestured at the town. "In the past?"

Pain flashed in her eyes, then smoldered into anger. She lifted her chin. "I'm going to find out the reason I'm here whether you want to join me or not."

He ground his teeth.

Patience. Be there for her.

Once again the thought pressed in on him like a weight. But he couldn't, because right now the only way he could see being there for her was by playing her game. And that meant saying he believed in her time-travel theory. Which he didn't. He wouldn't lie. So help him, he'd give no cause for anyone to distrust him, least of all Abigail.

"Fine." Abigail spat the word as though answering a question he hadn't asked. "You don't believe me. So go find a phone. Or a cop. Or whatever else you think will get us out of here. I'm going back to the hotel to try to figure out why she sent us to 1773." She flung her arms out, gaining the attention of several people passing by. "I refuse to stand here freezing while you wallow in male ego."

With a flare of her long dress, Abigail spun away from him and marched down the street.

Men. Men and their egos that refused to ask directions, refused to listen to a woman, and refused to believe they could ever *possibly* be wrong. A voice in the back of her head argued that she was being unfair to Evan. Given the situation, anyone would have a hard time believing they'd gone back in time.

Still.

She ignored the voice and strode purposely back toward the tavern. She almost didn't care if Evan followed her or not. He'd have to go back to the Green Dragon eventually. Where else could he go?

She glanced over her shoulder. A head taller than every person around him, Evan stared after her. But his feet didn't move. Furious with herself for looking back,

Abigail lifted her chin and walked faster.

He'd follow. Wouldn't he?

Unless she was wrong, and he was right. But in that case he'd find her at the tavern with a host of people wielding cell phones to show her the error of her ways. He wouldn't head home without her. Mad, though not entirely sure why she should be upset over Evan's arguably logical reaction, Abigail wrapped her arms around herself to shield herself from the biting wind.

Why Boston in the winter? Miserable cold was making her muscles tense and quivering. Causing her teeth to chatter. Miserable, rotten cold.

Not wanting to take the back door by the stable this time, Abigail approached the structure from the front. The tavern, or public house, as they were often called, looked more like a private residence than what she'd expected from a hotel-slash-pub. The two-story building, crafted from thick slats of wood, had a shingled roof, wide windows with diamond-shaped leaded glass, and sturdy shutters. Over the front door, a large copper dragon had turned a green patina from the sea air. Maybe that's where the place got the name. She swept open the door and stepped into a dimly lit foyer. The smells hit her immediately. Food, bread, and a myriad of other things she couldn't identify.

The next room offered an overflowing patronage of men in wigs or with long hair pulled back sitting over tall mugs of what she assumed to be alcohol. Other than the ones moving around with serving trays, no other women occupied the space dominated by men.

"Need help, Miss Martin?"

Abigail turned at the sound of her name and met the gaze of a distinguished-looking gentleman wearing a long coat with an abundance of ruffles around his neck. She placed him somewhere in his thirties.

How did he know her name?

Before she could answer, he produced a letter from his jacket pocket and held it out to her. "This arrived this morning with the Royal Mail."

This morning? She took the envelope. How would anyone know she would be here far enough in advance to mail a letter? The idea made her shiver.

The man must have noticed. "I'll send Mrs. Hugley to stoke your hearth. You seem to have caught a chill." He swept another assessing gaze over her. Probably wondering why she'd gone outside in a lady's fancy gown without a cloak.

"Thank you."

Nerves fluttering, she asked directions to the staircase and found her second-floor room again. She closed the door behind her and tried to draw a deep breath, but the dress she wore felt like an anaconda around her ribs.

Now what?

She'd stormed away from Evan expecting him to trail behind her and offer an apology. When he hadn't, she'd felt no joy at yet again being proved right when it came to the dependability—or rather, lack thereof—of men.

No matter. She'd be fine.

She sat at the small writing desk and examined the letter. A red wax seal had been stamped with a bold E. She slid her finger underneath and pulled out a sheet of thick paper.

Dear Abigail,

I'm guessing you are not quite as shocked by your adventure as most. You seemed to have an idea about what sort of excursion one might find when they come to visit me, and I sense you are a soul who welcomes the opportunity. However, you should know that the answers you find are likely not the answers you seek. I do not control the where or the when. Neither can you. To do so would give far too much power to human hands.

I am not often surprised by my guests, but I must admit I had no idea Mr. Blake would be joining you, though I am certain there must be a reason. The Conductor always has a plan, you see. You will have much to prove to one another, but when the time is done, you will discover a great treasure.

No signature. But the letter could only have come from Mrs. Easley. Satisfaction mingled with worry. This letter proved she'd been right about the time travel. Proved she was really in the past. Exciting, but also scary.

I do not control the where or the when. Neither can you.

The words ran in a loop through her head. She couldn't control the where or the when. Not good. That had been the entire point. *Now* Mrs. Easley told her—after Abigail had already made a jump, no less—that she wouldn't be able to manipulate the time warp house to send her to where she wanted to go.

Well. They'd see about that. Maybe Mrs. Easley didn't want Abigail to know the secret. But she'd figure it out.

Somehow.

She'd planned on figuring out the secret first, then using the house to teleport to Atlanta and witness the truth of her father's betrayal for herself. Maybe even undo some of her own mistakes. But before she'd even gotten to her room, the house had warped her here. She hadn't had a chance to discover anything.

There had to be a control panel to the time portal somewhere, didn't there? Someone had to know how to make it send her where she wanted to go.

A gnawing sense clamored for her attention—a sense that she was latching onto something she hoped to control in order to soothe the pain of all the things she couldn't control. She ignored the feeling.

God, I sure could—

No. She wouldn't pray. She didn't want to talk to Him, not after He'd allowed her to be deceived, humiliated, and taken advantage of. The least He could have done was stretch out His hand to catch her when she fell, but He hadn't even done that.

She wouldn't ask for His help now.

Something inside insisted she was being a child and only causing herself more pain by refusing the help of the Creator, but at the moment she didn't care. What other way did she have to express her grief than the silent treatment?

A knock at the door drew her from her contemplations. She opened it to find the woman who had come by earlier.

"I've come to build your fire, Miss Martin." This must be Mrs. Hugley. The same woman who had come by earlier to tell Evan about the patriot meeting. She dipped in a shallow sort of curtsy.

Abigail widened the door. "Thank you." Did she play along as though she belonged to this time or try to see if anyone would believe she'd come from another?

The woman busied herself poking at the fire glowing in the hearth. Despite the heat source, Abigail was still cold.

"Begging your pardon, Miss, but may I ask where you are visiting from?"

Huh. She thought a moment. "My family resides near the Mississippi River." Close enough, anyway. She couldn't very well mention a town that didn't exist. Besides, Mississippi was a river and maybe a territory, but certainly not a state in 1773.

The woman never looked up from the fire. "New Orleans?"

Near enough. "East of there, but yes."

"Is your family French?"

History. What did she remember of history? French and Indian War. Tension between the British and French. "I was born in the new land." Seemed a safe thing to say. "Why do you ask?"

"I've not heard anyone speak as you and Mr. Blake do. I find it interesting."

Her word choices or her accent? Probably both. She certainly didn't have the same slightly English sound of the colonist, and even though she'd never carried a thick Southern accent, even her mild one would stick out here. She turned the subject. "Can you tell me anything about the meeting?"

That question pulled Mrs. Hugley's attention from the fire. Her sharp eyes darted to the door, and uncertainty clouded her face.

"I assure you, we are the most loyal of patriots." Abigail offered the woman a smile.

The woman set the fire poker next to the hearth and took her time wiping her hands on the white apron around her waist. "Not many women would speak such to a stranger." Another assessing gaze.

This might be trickier than she thought. She had no idea how to act like a 1700s woman.

Mrs. Easley had said she would learn something

here. They seemed to be in Boston just prior to the infamous Boston Tea Party, but she couldn't fathom what any of that had to do with her learning her father's secrets. She plopped down on her chair.

"I may need some help bringing the men their drinks this evening," Mrs. Hugley said slowly. "Beneath a lady, I know, but—"

"I'd be happy to help." Abigail grinned, but the older woman didn't return her smile. She shifted in her seat. "I've served before." Waitressing at Outback and serving in an eighteenth century tavern couldn't be all that different.

The woman looked at her curiously again. A moment later she asked her leave and hurried out the door. Great. They didn't accuse weird people of being witches here, did they? Drown them or burn them at the stake for saying and doing odd things?

The idea brought a sense of terror, but she dismissed the feeling. No. She wouldn't have been brought here just to be killed. She was here to see or do something. And one of the most important events in history would be unfolding over the next few days.

A meeting of the great men who had founded America. A chance to see one of the early moments of the Revolution. Interesting.

But what in the world did any of that have to do with her?

Five

*J*mpossible. Women were completely impossible. Evan watched Abigail storm off and figured he'd best give her time to cool down. Besides, he needed to continue his quest for proof. The truth would solve everything.

Up ahead, a boy of around six or seven, dressed like a miniature version of the adults, swept bits of dirt and ice from in front of a shop door. Evan smirked. The adults might be able to keep up this sham, but a kid?

"Hello." Evan stopped a few steps away from the boy. He shoved his hands into his pockets. He wasn't accustomed to children, and certainly didn't approach children he didn't know.

The boy looked up. "Hello, sir. Looking for Mr. Rollard?"

Evan shook his head. "I was wondering if I might ask you a question."

The boy resumed his sweeping. "Yes, sir?"

"When you're not sweeping, what do you like to

do?" The kid gave him a funny look. Would the kid start screaming *stranger danger*? "Uh, what games do you like to play?"

The boy's light blond hair ruffled around the edges of a tiny black hat he'd pulled low over his ears. "I like hoops and scotch-hopper." His little face brightened, and his broom stilled. "Father says we'll get a good enough snow soon for sledding." Realizing he'd stopped his task, he furiously began sweeping again.

No video games. No TV shows. No mention of anything Evan would think a child would bring up. If asked a question like that, he'd spout off the truth, right?

"TV?"

The little guy tilted his head, clearly confused. He couldn't be that good of an actor, could he? Maybe.

"Never mind. Thanks." He moved down the street again.

Carts lumbered by, and horses whinnied. The cold wind plucked at his collar. He stepped around a pile of horse manure. Why didn't these people have sidewalks?

He stopped and scanned the people again, looking for someone he could convince to tell him the truth. A voice in his head warned he already knew the truth, but he refused to believe anything so…illogical.

An older boy, this one likely around twelve, carried an armload of chopped wood. Perfect. All kids had phones these days. He'd seen a study last week that said kids spent roughly nine hours a day on their devices. No way a boy his age wouldn't sneak one in his pocket.

Evan gained his side. "Need help?"

The boy cocked his head. "Sir?"

Feeling like even more of a weirdo, Evan tried for a friendly smile. "I'll help you carry your load if you'll answer some questions for me."

The kid thought a moment, then shrugged. "Mrs. Lawrence wants a stack at each hearth. Says storm's coming in tonight, but Lord only knows why she thinks so." He nodded over his shoulder. "Pile's in the back."

Evan glanced at the alleyway leading behind the tall, slender house. He'd meant he'd carry the load in the boy's arms. The front door opened, and the boy disappeared inside. He hesitated a moment then jogged down the narrow alley. Might as well keep himself busy while he gave Abigail time to settle. She'd see to reason once her emotions leveled out.

Or will you start to see her side instead?

The thought disturbed him, so he focused on the stack of chopped wood.

He gathered an armload and bustled to the front of the house, where a woman in a white apron gestured him inside and directed him to a room with a large dining table, a dozen cushioned chairs, and a massive fireplace. He stacked the wood on the hearth, casting glances at his surroundings.

The house looked like something he'd find in a

museum. How did people live in these stuffy rooms? Nothing here spoke of comfort. Of kicking off your shoes at the end of a hard day and watching the game. He'd hate to live here, even as an actor.

He nodded to the woman at the door as he stepped back into the foyer.

"Two more should do it, sir," the boy said as he bounded past, not even bothering to meet Evan's gaze.

Two more. He walked more slowly this time, watching the street. Every detail screamed authenticity. The accent of every person he'd met, the smells, the sounds of the horses.

He gathered another armload, rough splinters snagging on the nice fabric of his blue coat. The woman at the door dared a glance at him this time, her face clouded in confusion.

Did he seem out of place to her, or was she only wondering who he was?

The boy darted out of a room to his left and pointed at a doorway on the opposite side of the foyer. "Parlor's there. I'll get the last stack." Without waiting for a reply, he hurried outside again.

Evan looked at the woman standing guard over the door, wondering what part she played.

"I'm Evan Blake."

She glanced at him and dipped into a funny little curtsy thing. "Pleasure, sir." Suddenly her eyes widened. "Are you here to see the mistress?"

Right. It would make sense that he was here to visit the woman who owned the house. "Just helping the boy."

She looked confused but said nothing.

He stepped into a stuffy parlor. Squatty furniture. Heavy curtains over blurry glass windows. Another large fireplace glowed warmly, and after putting down the wood he took a second to stretch his fingers out to the embers. He hadn't realized how cold his fingers had gotten.

He waited a moment, but the boy didn't return. Better go find him. He didn't want the kid to run off before he got the chance to ask his questions. And since he'd done part of the boy's job, maybe he'd feel obligated to tell Evan the truth.

He dusted his hands on his pants and stepped back out into the hallway. The sandy-haired kid, all knees and elbows, appeared from another doorway to Evan's right a second later. The woman standing at the front handed the boy something and cast a questioning look at Evan.

Offering a friendly nod, Evan stepped past her and back out into the street. She closed the door behind the boy, her gaze lingering on Evan until the latch clicked.

"Thanks, mister." He pocketed a coin. "What did you want to ask?"

"Promise to be totally honest?"

The boy eyed him. "Aye, sir."

"Do you work here?"

He gave Evan a funny look, as though he'd just asked what color the sky was. "Mrs. Lawrence gives me a half-pence to do chores for her at times."

Stupid. He'd meant working in the reenactment in general, but he could see how the boy would mistake the question. "And what about when you aren't working here? Do you go to school? Ride the bus?"

The boy scowled. "I finished my primers last year." He puckered his mouth. "What's a bus?"

Evan ground his teeth. "The truth, please. I need to get out of this nightmare."

The boy took a step back.

Evan grabbed his arm. "Fifty bucks if you let me use your phone."

He snatched his arm away and shook his head. "You're talking nonsense, mister." With another shake of his head he turned and dashed away.

No. No, no.

He repeated the word to himself all the way back to the tavern, the denial pounding with each thud of his boots on the cobbled street. Was Abigail right? Had they really traveled back in time? Why? How?

The large building teemed with people who darted in and out of the door underneath a metal dragon. Men, mostly, but a few women as well. All dressed in long gowns and most wearing their hair in intricate curls. One, a dark-haired girl he guessed to be no more than sixteen, offered him a coy smile before the older man holding her elbow pulled her away.

Evan stepped inside the noisy establishment. Maybe he'd knocked his skull or something when he passed out and all of this was in his head. Made more sense than time travel.

Lost in thought, Evan started when a man grabbed his shoulder.

"Mr. Blake?"

Evan blinked at the shorter man dressed in a fancier version of the costumes—or period era clothing—than many of the men on the street.

The man glanced behind Evan, but no one else currently stood in the front room. "This way, sir. We'll hold our discussion in the basement."

The basement? Evan drew his head back. No way was he going to a basement with this weirdo. "Where's Abigail?"

The man gestured for Evan to follow him. "Miss Martin? She volunteered her services. If you'll follow me, please."

Her services? What did that mean? What had she gotten into now? He followed the man down the hallway, senses on guard. He could take this guy if he had to.

The man opened a door that led to a narrow set of steps lit only by a droopy candle on the wall. Evan hesitated. This was how horror movies went. Follow the stranger down into the dark basement to get murdered.

Laugher erupted from below. At least he wasn't going to the basement alone. Still. Could be an ambush. Or a cult meeting.

His guide was already halfway down the steps, undeterred by the gloom. A woman's laugh joined the sounds of the men.

Abigail?

Definitely her. He plodded down the steps. Whatever was going on, it didn't sound like she was in any danger.

The room at the bottom was exactly what he would expect of a colonial basement. Brick floor and walls. Low ceiling. Candles glowing from numerous stands, the thick wax dripping on the floor.

Abigail, wearing a simple dress with a white apron tied over the drab brown fabric, stood at a table, laughing with a man wearing buckle shoes, hose, and long hair tied with a ribbon. The woman who had come to Abigail's room earlier and told him about the meeting poured liquid into tankards around the table.

One of the men, an older fellow by the looks of his gray hair, turned to study Evan with probing brown eyes. He wore a wine-colored coat with a white shirt that looked like it might choke him. He had a rounded face and a prominent nose.

Other men crowded the table, all dressed in similar clothing. Long coats with gold embroidery and lots of buttons. Knee-length pants and white hose. Weird. So weird.

Slowly, he realized the room had grown quiet and everyone stared at him. He cleared his throat. The man who had brought him down raised a hand to the group.

"Gentlemen, allow me to introduce Mr. Evan Blake of the Georgia colony. A mason, he has come to fellowship with us this eve." He gestured to the table. "Mr. Adams, Mr. Hancock, Mr. Revere and Mr. Otis," he said, indicating each man in turn.

Evan's mouth dried. Was this some kind of joke? Revere? Hancock?

He'd been invited to a meeting with some of the founding fathers? His eyes locked on Abigail. She smiled.

"The Sons of Liberty." The words escaped his parched throat like sandpaper across a rusty pipe. Impossible.

The man who'd led him down clasped him on the shoulder. "Precisely, my boy. Join us."

Dazed, Evan took the seat the man offered. Someone called him Mr. Warren. Not a familiar name. Not like Revere and Adams. He smirked, despite the situation. Where was Washington?

The mirth died instantly. Fearing he could no longer claim all these people were pretending, he met each of their gazes. The founding fathers.

His head swam.

What in the world was happening?

Poor Evan looked positively pale. Abigail had never seen him so wide-eyed. He took the deer in headlights cliché to a new level. Bless his heart. She was sure the current circumstance had him grasping at the frayed edges of his logical explanations. Sooner or later, he had to see time travel was the only thing that made sense.

"Mankind are governed more by their feelings than by reason," Samuel Adams said, tapping a finger on the table.

She could hardly believe it. Men from history. The leaders of the Revolution. What would they think about America as she knew it? And here she was, right in the middle of history unfolding. These men were discussing what to do about the ships that refused to leave the harbor.

The Dartmouth, the Eleanor, and the Beaver had arrived in Boston Harbor, and the colonists had demanded that the tea they carried be returned to England. Hutchinson, the governor, refused, as did the ships' owners.

"And what says Roth?" one of the men asked— maybe his name was Mr. Otis.

Adams shook his head. "He refused. On the account that his ships would be broadsided by the Somerset and Boyne. Warships. I told Roth that his ship must sail back to London. The people of Boston and the neighboring towns absolutely require and expect it."

"Something must be done," Hancock said. "Men stand ready."

"Yet they will not act for fear of being known." Adams glowered, his expression calling such men cowards.

"Dressed like Indians," Abigail mused. That must be why the Sons of Liberty had dressed their members like Mohawk tribesmen with their faces covered in soot and war paint.

"What now?" Samuel Adams turned his seat to stare at her.

She gulped. "Um, you said something about a disguise, didn't you, sir?" He continued to stare at her. "To, uh, make men more willing to participate if they can remain anonymous."

His eyebrows lifted, and one side of his mouth tugged up.

Mrs. Hugley appeared at her shoulder. "Fetch the plates, miss, if you will."

"What? Oh."

Mrs. Hugley gestured to the stairs, her face pinched with embarrassment. Maybe Abigail wasn't supposed to talk to the men. But it wasn't as if she'd altered history or anything. The Boston Tea Party was famous for the participants dressing up like Indians.

Of course, Mrs. Hugley wouldn't know that. How

could she know Adams would come up with the idea on his own? Abigail probably sounded crazy.

She tried to catch Evan's eye, but he was staring at John Hancock as if he'd seen a ghost.

Mrs. Hugley tugged on her arm. "The meal, please."

Hating to miss out on the conversation but knowing her service was the only reason she'd been permitted to be there, Abigail scampered toward the stairs.

Up above, she found her way down the hallway and into the kitchen. As soon as she opened the door, blessed heat washed over her. She'd been so enamored with the men downstairs that she hadn't even noticed how chilly the basement was.

Her shoulders relaxed. The kitchen smelled of bread and meat, and women's chatter hung on the air. Three women dusted in flour kneaded dough on a thick wooden table. A massive arched fireplace held two large caldrons. The black pots bubbled over the flames. A churn and various other objects she wasn't familiar with crowded the corners by the fireplace.

Suddenly, a stout woman with reddened cheeks hefted a tray at her. "You serving below, girl?"

"Oh." She barely grasped the tray as the woman thrust it into her stomach. "Yes."

"Then get on with you. Take the soup, then you can come back for the bread and cheese."

Abigail gripped the sides of the wood as the woman turned away and resumed her conversation with the other women.

Man. The tray was heavy. Abigail strained against the weight. And here she'd thought herself in decent shape. She lumbered to the door, careful not to trip on a cat that darted right in front of her. How awful would that have been?

She glanced behind her, but none of the women seemed interested in helping her with the door. Fine. She could do it on her own.

Using her foot, she nudged open the door and stepped out into the hallway. A girl with an empty tray barreled her direction, and Abigail sidestepped to get out of her way. Stew sloshed over the side of one of the ceramic bowls.

Yikes.

Her boss would've had her hide for being so clumsy, but plastic trays weren't the same as this heavy wooden one. Even with only six bowls, the thing felt like it weighed fifty pounds. Muscles already beginning to burn, Abigail held her head high and stepped carefully down the long hall and back to the door that led to the basement.

The steep, narrow stairs daunted her. One at a time. Breathe. She coached herself one slow, careful step at a time until she reached the bottom without incident.

The men were still arguing over the best course of action. Adams said something about how they must rouse men to indignation if they were to force the ships to comply.

Several of the others nodded. She locked eyes with Evan. Bigger than the other men, he stood out like a draft horse among thoroughbreds. And he looked as uncomfortable as a canary in a cat house. She offered a smile he didn't return.

Poor Evan. He was having an even harder time than—

Her foot caught on something. The weight in her arms pulled her forward. She scrambled, churning her feet in a desperate attempt to keep her balance. She wavered. Teetered.

Momentum overtook her. In slow motion she felt herself falling forward. Felt the tray slipping from her hands.

Someone shouted. Abigail hit the ground with a thud and a clatter.

Horrified, she looked up.

John Hancock and Paul Revere were covered head-to-lap in steaming soup.

Six

*N*ot good. Evan scrambled from his seat, slid on spilled carrots and onions, and dropped to Abigail's side where she lay sprawled on the floor.

"Are you okay?" He gripped her arm. She trembled beneath his fingers.

She blinked at him, her beautiful face red with embarrassment. "I'm so sorry!"

He lifted her to her feet. "It was an accident."

The men doused in their supper rose. They offered small bows to the room and then disappeared up the stairs. Abigail dropped her head, tears streaming down her face.

"I'm so sorry," she said again, this time to the room in general.

Mrs. Hugley rushed over with a towel she'd produced from thin air and began furiously mopping the floor, mumbling something under her breath.

Evan turned Abigail away from the table and wrapped an arm around her waist. "Come on. Let's get you upstairs."

"I dumped food all over the founding fathers!" She leaned her head into his shoulder. "I'm the worst time-traveler ever." The last words were so soft he barely heard her. Hopefully no one else had noticed her comments.

They had to walk single file up the narrow staircase, but at the top he took her arm again. "I interrogated two children today," he said lightly.

As he'd hoped, she immediately stopped brushing at her apron and turned flashing eyes on him. "You did what?" The mixture of surprise and annoyance in her voice was nearly comical.

He grinned. Back to feisty Abigail. "I thought I could get one of them to give me a phone. Or at least tell me his favorite video game."

Evan guided her to the main staircase, ignoring the stares of colonists in the foyer.

"And?" The sharp word jabbed him.

"And…" He cleared his throat. "I guess you're right. These aren't actors."

Her triumphant smile sent a shock of heat through him. Did she have any idea how gorgeous she was with confidence painting her lips?

The smile faltered and slid away. "And I dumped stew all over them." She practically groaned the words and clomped the rest of the way up the staircase.

He waited until they were enclosed in her room

before he spoke again. "You didn't mean to."

She made a sour face as though that didn't matter at all. "Mortifying. I won't be allowed down there again." She grabbed the chair at the writing desk and plopped down, crossing her arms.

There wasn't another chair in the room, and he wasn't going to sit on her bed, so he chose to lean his shoulder against the wall. "It's not that bad."

Her lips puckered as though she were about to stick her tongue out at him like she had when they were teens, but then they flattened into a line of frustration.

"So what do we do now?" Evan asked. "I don't really want to be stuck in the land of panty hose."

"What?" she barked a laugh. "Panty hose?"

Evan gestured to his lower legs, and Abigail rolled her eyes. "No electricity, Abs. No proper bathrooms."

Her eyes widened, but she quickly tried to hide her horror.

"No hot showers. No internet. No—"

"I get it."

The dim room cast her face in shadows, and he glanced at the fireplace. He should probably see about getting her some more wood. She hated to be cold and, it was already getting chilly in here. Candlelight was fine for romantic dinners and all, but it did practically nothing for decent lighting. Maybe he could find her one of those old oil lamps. They had those, right?

He slid his gaze back to Abigail. She still watched

him as though he had answers. Evan turned out his palm. "So...what do we do?"

"How should I know?"

"You're the time-travel expert. How did your friend get home?"

"I don't know."

He pushed off the wall. He hadn't considered Abigail wouldn't be able to get them out of here. Once he'd realized she was right about the time travel, he'd just assumed she would know how to reverse it. "No clues? Nothing?"

"There was one thing." Her eyebrows drew together.

The pause drew out so long that Evan prompted, "Well?"

Abigail looked around the room. At the fireplace, the lumpy bed, the wood walls. Anywhere but at him. Finally, she shrugged. "I don't think it's going to help any."

They had to start somewhere. He struggled to keep annoyance from his voice. "What thing?"

She pulled a paper from a pocket she had hidden underneath her apron and held it out to him.

He unfolded the thick parchment and scanned the contents. "Who wrote this?"

"Mrs. Easley, I guess."

I had no idea Mr. Blake would be joining you.

The line made his skin crawl. She hadn't meant to

send him back in time? Did that mean he couldn't get home? If he wasn't supposed to be here, did that mean he was some kind of stowaway without return passage? Would Abigail suddenly disappear and leave him stranded?

"I don't know what she means about what we're supposed to learn." Abigail's eyes searched his face, clearly still doubting he believed in time travel after all.

What was it about him that caused people to doubt what he said? Even Abigail, who should know him better than anyone doubted what he said. Was he really that untrustworthy?

Forcing his annoyance aside, he focused on the only clues they had. Mrs. Easley hadn't exactly kidnapped them, but she had sent them to Colonial Boston without their—or at least his—consent. The letter indicated they had to learn something. Maybe once they learned whatever information she was after, she'd zap them back home.

The idea sounded incredibly insane, but what else did he have to go on? They were in the same tavern as the Sons of Liberty at the brink of the Boston Tea Party. No way was that coincidence. So they must be looking for information on the founding fathers.

Thanks to Abigail's little mishap and him leaving with her, they probably wouldn't be invited near those men again. Still. He probably should try.

Fourth and twenty, but he had to go for it.

Abigail stared at her hands, apparently lost in her own thoughts. Evan cleared his throat. "You good?"

Her gaze slammed into his. "With what?"

"Are you ready to go back downstairs? If we're supposed to learn something, I'm guessing those men are our best bet."

She clutched the fabric of her skirt. "I can't go back down there."

"Because of one little spill?"

"Little?" She spat the word. "I was humiliated."

"No more than Hancock and Revere." He grinned.

But rather than gaining a laugh, his words caused tears to spring into her eyes. They slid down her cheeks as silent testaments to his callous idiocy. He dropped to his knee by her side. The old pain in his kneecap flared at the jolt, but he ignored it. "I was trying to be funny." He grimaced. "Sorry."

She swiped tears. "I make a mess of everything."

He grabbed her hand and rubbed his thumb over her knuckles. "No, you don't."

She tried to pull away, but he held firm. "How would you know?"

The bite in her tone felt like cleats to the stomach. Did nothing he said matter? Remembering that he was supposed to be trying for patience, Evan kept as much sweetness in his voice as he could. "I know we lost touch, but that doesn't mean I don't know you." Words he wanted to say froze in his throat. Now wasn't the time. He took a different tact. "And I know you to be a smart, capable person. Tripping and falling doesn't change that."

"I got fired." The words shot out of her mouth like cannonballs.

What? The sudden twist in topic threw him, and he took a second to catch up. Her job in Atlanta. The one she'd run off to when she'd left him like a discarded memory. He squeezed her fingers. "What happened?"

Glistening tears spilled over her lower lashes. "I found out the truth about my father and didn't take it well. Exploded, you might say, in the middle of the breakroom."

Wow.

"At his birthday party."

Evan cringed.

"With all the partners."

Oh boy.

She squeezed her eyes shut. "I called him all kinds of names. He fired me. Told me to get out. Evicted me from the apartment he'd given me. Took the car. He won't answer my calls." Her shoulders shook with a wobbly breath. "That's why I came back. That's what happened in Atlanta."

That explained why she'd called his parents out of the blue when they hadn't heard from her in months. Without her father, Abigail had no remaining family. "What did you find out about your father that set you off?"

Her eyes narrowed. "It doesn't matter."

What? She brought it up, but now she looked at him like he was trying to pry a secret out of her. Whatever she'd found out, it obviously shook her. But why didn't she want to tell him?

She dropped her gaze and stared at their clasped hands. Something in the air shifted between them. A sensation he couldn't describe tingled through him like a jolt of adrenaline.

"Why did you leave Ocean Springs?" He caught and held her gaze. His question hadn't come out quite right. He knew she'd taken the job at her dad's advertising firm as a graphic designer. "I mean why did you leave so suddenly? You missed the going-away party my mom was going to surprise you with. You weren't supposed to leave for four more days, and you just…ran out on us. I tried to call you several times, but…" He shrugged.

She studied him. And suddenly stiffened. Oh no. Now she'd clam up, and he'd never get the truth. She'd avoided every attempt he'd made at getting her to talk about why she'd avoided him and his family. She started to pull away from him. So much for the moment of honesty he'd thought they'd been having. The coldness she'd shown him when he'd first picked her up from the airport returned. It seemed almost as though, in the craziness of their predicament, she'd forgotten she hated him, but now she remembered the feeling with vengeance.

And he couldn't stand that.

"I have feelings for you." The words dropped like a bomb, sending shards of tension slicing through the room. Not the best way to tell her. Certainly not the most romantic way.

She stared at him.

He hurried on. "After you left, I couldn't stop thinking about you. I realized I missed you. And not just as my friend. You were always the perfect girl for me even if I was too dumb to see it. But I told myself to get over my feelings. You had a new life and opportunities in Atlanta and you obviously didn't want to hear from me. It took time, but I finally thought I'd moved on. Let you go. But then I found out you were coming back and…"

Was she even breathing? She still stared at him, expression unreadable.

Evan sucked in a breath. "All those feelings came charging back."

Her mouth opened, then closed again. Her tongue slid over her lips. "You were always a good friend, Evan." She cleared her throat. "Mostly."

Friend. The word he'd expected yet dreaded. He'd forever be benched on the friend team. She didn't want more. Hurt swelled, but he forced it away. He still deserved the truth. "Why did you leave like that?"

"It doesn't matter." She tugged away from him and stood, brushing her skirts as though doing so would get the specks of stew off her apron. "You're right. We better get back down there."

Now she wanted to go back? Face what she considered humiliation rather than discuss what he'd said? What was he, the lesser of two evils? He ground his teeth. Fine.

He'd go back down to the basement and see what he could learn from the men. He'd had enough of the past. Time to go home. He'd make sure they got back.

One way or another.

Heart raw and flayed, Abigail watched Evan stalk out the door. She should follow him, but she couldn't seem to get her feet to respond. Her mind pulsed with one consuming revelation.

Evan had feelings for her. Feelings that went beyond friendship? No. She couldn't believe that. He didn't know the truth about her. Or realize that she knew the truth about him.

She'd suggested they go back to the meeting, but only because she'd been searching for a way out of the conversation. A way to stop him from saying things they would both eventually regret. Because once he realized she knew what he'd said about her, there'd be no going back. Her heart wrenched at the memory.

Abigail? You don't want her, man. She's six kinds of crazy.

Closing the door to her room, she let the pain of that reality overtake her before she let herself be stupid enough to think his words now could mean anything.

He'd looped his arm over the shoulder of a curvy blonde while his football buddies all laughed. He hadn't known she was there. Hadn't known she'd gone up to Mississippi State that night to surprise him. His words and his friends' laughter had torn her tender heart to shreds. Her best friend. The one she'd trusted enough to share her secrets with. The only person she'd felt like she could be herself around apparently thought her true self was "six kinds of crazy." Crazy, just like her mother had always said. Crazy Abigail coming up with wild theories. Incapable of keeping her head on straight.

Knowing his thoughts had always secretly matched her mother's had stoked her insecurities and set flame to her self-doubts.

Devastated, she'd left the party and driven to Atlanta that night. She'd refused to answer his calls. Couldn't stand to hear his voice. As the months passed, she'd considered answering his texts. Or his mom's phone calls. But the longer she stayed away, the easier they'd both become to ignore.

Until her world fell apart and Evan's parents had been the only people she could call. The only parental figures of wisdom and kindness she could trust. And they'd sent *him* to the airport. Why? When she'd specifically asked to see his mother? Shaking her head, Abigail refused to let herself dissolve into sobs.

Instead, she focused on her anger.

Her father was a liar. Her mother was fourteen months in the grave. She had no job, no home, and was now stuck more than two hundred years in the past.

Then again, she couldn't get much farther away from her problems than 1773. Except of course for the one who had time-hopped with her. She groaned.

Her heart tightened with an aching pressure, the kind that would demand release. She'd learned years ago the best way to let her emotions bleed was with pen and paper. When she felt this way, she wrote all the words she needed to get out, then burned them to ash. That way she could say everything she needed to without wounding other people. Or facing her mother's wrath. Somehow, releasing the anger on the page and then watching that page burn brought peace.

The practice had often kept her from spewing words she shouldn't. If she didn't release everything she was feeling for Evan Blake now, she would end up shouting the hurt at him later. Then she wouldn't even have a fractured friendship to rely on in the middle of this mess.

Hating that she desperately wanted Evan's company while at the same time loathing his presence for all the painful memories he stirred, she reminded herself that she'd forgiven him. At least, she'd thought she had.

Back when she'd thought she'd never see him again.

At the writing desk Abigail pulled a few sheets of paper—thick pieces she could still see the fibers in—from the drawer. A sharpened feather sat neatly by the stack. A quill? Beside it, a tiny inkpot. She wrinkled her nose. That would be difficult.

Better than nothing.

She dipped the cut tip of the quill pen into the jar of ink and made a mark at the top of the page. Not bad. She could do that. With a sloppy script, spatters of ink droplets, and a few illegible words, Abigail scrawled her heart onto the page.

Evan Blake. How could you?

She kept writing, line after line until the page was filled. Then she grabbed another sheet of paper and kept going. With each scratch of the pen, her burden lightened until the anger and hurt transferred from her heart to the page. Finally, her emotions spent, she leaned back and sighed.

Was she coming or not? Evan waited at the bottom of the main stairway, but Abigail still hadn't taken up her own suggestion to return to the meeting. He should have known. She'd only wanted to get rid of him.

Fine.

Something told him to give her a moment rather than go back and force her to walk with him, so he continued through the main floor of the building and to the doorway leading to the basement.

He waited again. Still no Abigail.

Evan brushed his annoyance away. Maybe she had to return to the kitchen first for something.

The voices of the men sounded down the basement stairwell, so Evan carefully descended the steep stairs. Conversation stilled as he entered the room.

Mr. Warren, the owner of the tavern, stepped close. "Miss Martin? How fares she?"

"Fine…uh, sir. Just a bit embarrassed."

The man nodded and gestured for him to take a seat at the table with the remaining men. He cut a glance at the doorway. She should have been here by now.

The men welcomed him back to the table where they'd finished their meals. Mrs. Hugley gathered discarded plates and bowls. She shot him a loaded glance, but he pretended not to notice. Apparently, he wouldn't be sampling any colonial cooking tonight. Not unless Abigail swallowed her pride and returned with another tray of food. Which he doubted.

The men had a weird, formal way of speaking. Evan focused on the sentence patterns and accents while trying to understand what they planned. From what he could gather, Samuel Adams was the ringleader of this operation. No news there. So far, Evan didn't pick up any information Mrs. Easley couldn't get from an elementary school history book.

"It does not take a majority to prevail," Adams said, his voice sharp with conviction. "But rather an irate, tireless minority, keen on setting brushfires of freedom in the minds of men."

Despite knowing the outcome where these men could not, he felt his emotions stir. Adams was right. How often in history had circumstances changed because one small group refused to be disregarded? An odd sense of patriotism enveloped him.

"And you, Blake. What say you?"

Evan smiled. "You have my wholehearted agreement."

The declaration seemed to please the men, who gave him nods of approval and lifted glasses. A rap at the door announced the return of Hancock and Revere. Dressed in clean clothes almost identical to the ones Abigail had splattered in soup, they returned to the table and jumped right into the conversation about port masters, the governor, and unloading cargo as though they hadn't missed any of the conversation.

Mrs. Hugley rushed forward to offer them a meal, but they waved her away with words of thanks, and she returned to a small table by the wall to wait. Great. Still no supper for him.

The men continued their lively discussion about the ships in the harbor, the actions that could be taken, and what needed to be done. They spoke with such fervor. Such passion. When had he ever been *that* focused on a goal? Football hardly compared to the freedom of a nation. Though bigger in stature than all of these men, they somehow made Evan feel dwarfed.

Despite their stirring conversation, however, Evan heard nothing unexpected. How would he know what information Mrs. Easley sought? Maybe she wanted an account of the actual events to test them against what she knew from history. He'd try to cram as much of their heated discussion into his brain as he could manage.

When he thought his brain could hold no more, Mr. Warren called the evening to a close.

The men rose and shook hands, promises of finding a resolution "on the morrow" echoed by all. In the midst of the confusing conversation, Evan had somehow agreed to attend tomorrow's gathering at a place called the Liberty Tree.

He finished shaking hands with the men who'd spurred America to freedom, then followed them out of the basement.

Despite what had to be a late hour, he had one more confusing conversation to unravel tonight. And he would do it, even if he had to corner Abigail to make it happen.

Time to send the words crumbling to ashes. Feeling lighter, Abigail turned to the hearth to sacrifice her pain to the flames. Ugh. Not again.

The small hearth once again held little more than a few glowing embers. Gracious, how quickly did the wood burn out around here? Seeing the dying fire alerted her body to the chill in the room, and Abigail shivered. These people needed to figure out better insulation.

Maybe she could get the heat going again. She grabbed a poker on the hearth and jabbed the metal tip into the embers. A small flame flared but quickly died again.

She'd better get more fuel. After replacing the poker, she headed to the door. Where would she find wood? Mrs. Hugley had started the fire and seemed the logical person to ask, but Abigail had no desire to face the woman right now.

The kitchen would be her best bet. She hurried down the stairs, keeping an eye out for Evan, Mrs. Hugley, and any of the founding fathers and was pleased when she didn't see them. They must still be talking in the basement. How mad would Evan be that she hadn't come downstairs?

Only two women remained in the kitchen. They

both looked up as she entered. One swept while the other wiped flour from the long wooden table. Delicious warmth from the hearth wrapped comforting fingers around Abigail's shoulders, and her tense muscles relaxed.

The woman sweeping—the cook who'd thrust the tray into Abigail's middle—stilled her broom and gave Abigail an assessing gaze. "Need something?"

"Where do I get more wood for my room?"

The women exchanged a look. The cook put a hand on her hip and seemed as though she was about to fire off a retort but quickly changed her mind. Her face softened, and she gave a nod. "I'll have a kitchen boy fetch more for you, miss."

Abigail shook her head. She didn't want to make a poor child do a task she could do on her own. "I got it."

The women exchanged another look. Abigail shifted. Did they think she was super weird? Probably, but what did that matter?

"'Tis not a task for a lady to suffer, miss. Will take us but a few moments, if you'd be so kind as to wait."

"No need to make someone else do what I can accomplish myself."

The cook looked like she would protest again, but Abigail straightened to her full height and lifted her chin.

The act seemed to work because the cook bobbed her head. "Certainly, miss. As you wish." She gestured to a door in the rear of the kitchen. "We keep a wood stack close there."

Abigail thanked her and hurried outside. The cold day had dissolved into a frigid night, and the wind nearly stole her breath. How much wood could she carry to create a good blaze? She certainly wanted more than the tiny amount Mrs. Hugely had brought, and she could definitely carry more than some poor kid, at least enough to keep burning through the night. She refused to try to sleep in the frigid temperatures, even if she had to pile all the blankets on the floor and sleep next to the fireplace.

A large pile of cut and chopped wood stood neatly stacked just outside the back door, as the cook had said. Abigail gathered as much as she could in her arms, but it wasn't enough. What about her stained apron? Good thing she'd been too wrapped up in her writing to take it off. Setting the pieces down, she crouched and folded the bottom of the long apron to create a type of hammock. That should work.

Holding the edges with one hand, she filled her apron with as much wood as she could carry and then struggled to her feet. Her fingers burned with cold, and her ears stung from the wind. Maybe this was *too* much. But how quickly would the fuel diminish? She certainly didn't want to face the choice of getting more wood or freezing at three in the morning. Struggling against the awkward weight, she scuttled to the door.

With both hands full, she couldn't turn the knob. She kicked at the bottom of the door with her foot. Teeth chattering, she waited. No one came. She kicked again.

If she ended up dropping all of this while trying to open the door—

Light flooded the yard, and the young woman who'd been wiping the table appeared. She blinked at Abigail. "Miss? Do you require assistance?"

"No," Abigail barked. "Just let me in."

The woman scrambled out of the way as Abigail charged inside. Stupid cold. Why did people live in places like this? If she had her way, she'd move to Hawaii or some other tropical island and never see a flake of snow in her life.

Fueled by her desire to get back to her room, warm herself by the flames, and watch her words go up in smoke, Abigail struggled up the rear stairs she guessed the workers used. Thankfully, both the stairwell and the hallway remained empty.

Only a few more steps.

The door to her room stood open. Her pulse kicked up. Hadn't she closed it? Frowning, she quickened her steps as much as she could with the weight pressing against her middle.

And then she remembered… Her pages! She'd left them on the desk.

Seven

What a weird night. Who would have thought Evan would meet the man famous for shouting the British were coming and the guy who would famously scrawl his name in giant letters across the bottom of the Declaration of Independence? Even with such unimaginable circumstances, Evan's thoughts kept returning to Abigail.

She'd purposely remained vague about whatever he'd done to upset her, but there was no denying he'd landed in the friend zone. Though, given how she'd refused to talk to him for the past year, maybe he should count himself lucky to have even made that cut. Things could be worse. Still, he'd tried to tell her he'd changed. Tried to show her he wasn't the same jerk he'd been in college. How could he prove he could be trusted?

He could start with being there for her. Whether she wanted him or not.

With that thought in mind, he strode up the main staircase. A few candles glowed softly, giving him just enough light to make his way down the hall. Hopefully she hadn't gone to bed yet. He had no way of knowing the time.

He knocked on Abigail's door.

No answer.

He knocked again. "Abs? Can I come in?"

Nothing. A sudden thought grabbed him and squeezed the air from his lungs. She hadn't disappeared back to the future, had she? Fighting panic, he thrust the door open.

Empty. The bed was still made. The fire had dwindled to nothing more than a faint glow in the hearth.

"Abigail?" He strode inside.

Papers on the desk snagged his attention. He walked closer and saw his name at the top of the first page. He snatched the paper. She'd left him a letter? Before what? Going back home or running away to who-knew-where in the middle of a dangerous time? His eyes devoured the first scrawled words.

Evan Blake. How could you?

The script was hard to read, but he slowly made out the scratches and deciphered one painful line after another.

How could you say something like that? And what's worse, you don't even know how you found the one thing that could destroy me and used it as a joke with your friends. Not that you would care, I guess. You are the perfect guy. The star athlete. Mr. Popular. You chew girls' hearts up and spit them out, one after another. I won't be one of them.

But then, I am six kinds of crazy, so who am I to say what I'll do? Crazy. Maybe I am.

What was she talking about? His eyebrows pulled together in concentration, each jab lifting off the page to punch him in the gut.

But what would you know about the terrible things that can happen to make a person a bit crazy? You wouldn't. Not with your perfect life. You have no idea what it's like to not be enough. Never, ever, enough. Not even to the people who are supposed to love you the most.

The last word trailed off the bottom edge of the page. He set it down and picked up the next. This one seemed to be some kind of poem rather than a letter.

When did Abigail write poetry? Maybe he didn't know her as well as he'd thought. These words were scratched in the same splattered ink, but he was getting faster at reading.

Enough is becoming a four-letter word instead of six. Never is enough…enough.

Not enough time, not enough patience, not enough energy. Never smart enough, good enough, or pretty enough.

I wait, always on the edge. Waiting for that moment when you see through me. For you to see that I'm not enough for you. Someday you will see me as I do. And that someday, enough will be enough for you, too.

So I hide the truth of me. I smother it and try to keep it locked away in the deepest recesses of my heart.

The painful reality remains. Waiting, always waiting. Waiting for you to see what I see. To see that I am not, cannot, be enough.

I've had enough of this feeling, and yet it never goes away. Each day, pecking, pecking, pecking at me. Like ravens with black beaks and sharp claws. Pecking at walls that are supposed to hide what you are not supposed to see.

Pecking until the truth of me breaks free. And you see what I see.

Today you saw through me and you knew. You knew that I was not enough.

And you walked away.

He stared at the page, heart twisting. Abigail wrote this? Saw herself as not enough? Enough for who? Him or someone else?

Was he the one who'd walked away?

A squeak sounded behind him, followed by a bump and clatter. Evan whirled.

And found Abigail staring at him, a pile of wood around her feet.

No! Evan held the pages she'd wanted to burn, his eyes holding all the pain she'd planned to exile to the flames. She launched herself over the wood she'd spilled in her shock, stumbled, and finally righted herself.

Stormy blue eyes darted back to the page, then again to her, confusion and hurt swirling in their depths.

He held the words that had leaked out of her heart, never meant for any eyes other than her own. Meant for the flames. Why hadn't she taken them with her? Because she hadn't expected him to trespass on her privacy. Shame roared into anger.

She charged across the room and snatched the paper from Evan's hand.

"What are you doing in here? Poking through my private things?"

He folded his hands behind him and stared down at her, thoughts churning behind a guarded expression.

"This is private," she snapped. "What possessed you to think you could barge in here and read my innermost thoughts?"

Sadness tightened his full mouth and caused small lines at the corners of his eyes. Despite her fury, Abigail's heart twisted. She hadn't meant to hurt him. Not even if he deserved to feel the pain he'd caused her.

Evan opened his mouth. Closed it again. The muscles of his square jawline ticked, but he remained infuriatingly silent.

Abigail stomped her foot. "Say something!"

Evan's shoulders lifted and fell with a long breath. "I'm sorry."

She glared at him. "That's it? Just *sorry*? Nothing to say for *why* you barged in here?"

His Adam's apple bobbed. "I thought you'd disappeared. Then I…I saw my name and thought you'd left me a letter."

Under any other circumstances, she'd consider his explanation a lame excuse. Now, however, his actions could conceivably be justified. Still. He should have stopped reading once he realized she hadn't been writing to him.

Not directly, anyway.

Fine. She *had* been writing to him. And okay, sure, she was mature enough to admit that, if she'd been in his shoes, she'd probably have kept reading as well. She'd discovered a fatal flaw in her self-therapy. *Always* keep the evidence with her until she could feed the flames.

Abigail groaned, her anger melting into a toxic mixture of humiliation and guilt. "You weren't supposed to see that."

He continued to watch her, unnervingly silent. What was he thinking? How crazy she was? Why not say out loud what he really thought? She couldn't take him standing there, judging her without the decency of letting her in on his condemnations.

She flung out her hands. "I do that, all right? I write things down. Get them off my chest. Then I burn them. Crazy. I know." Her chest constricted, her breaths coming in ragged gasps.

Evan's steady gaze tore apart her composure.

She snatched the other page from the desk. Had he read everything? Heat welled inside her, dispelling the cold. Barely thinking, she flung the pages into the nearly dead coals. One edge smoldered but refused to light. Abigail snatched the poker and jabbed at the paper, shoving it further into the coals.

Evan grabbed her shoulders. She stiffened. Gently, he took the fire poker from her hand and rested it on the hearth. He turned her around to face him.

The room was mostly dark, save for the candles burning on the desk. With the puny light behind him, she could barely make out his features, but she could feel the regret radiating from him.

"I'm sorry," he said again. "I'm sorry for reading your papers. I'm sorry for whatever I did to hurt you. I'm sorry that I didn't swallow my pride and drive to Atlanta and demand you see me after you left. I'm sorry I never told you that I love you."

All the air left her lungs. She didn't hear right. Couldn't have. He meant he loved her like family. Like his parents did. Nothing else. Of course not anything romantic.

They had been friends, once. In another life. High school seemed like so long ago now. That close friendship had strained during college and broken soon after. They were adults now. Different people.

He didn't know her anymore.

Maybe she didn't know him either.

"I was a jerk back then. Full of pride and ego." He ran a finger down her cheek, and she shivered. But not from the cold. "I shouldn't have let you go without a fight. I'm sorry that I never let you know how much you mean to me." His voice lowered until it was husky. Almost raw. "I never meant to cause you any pain. I wish you could trust me and that you didn't doubt that I've told you the truth."

Tears burned in her eyes. She buried the vulnerability underneath a snarky tone. "But I'm crazy, remember?"

"What are you talking about?"

She shook her head. If he didn't realize the truth after reading what she'd practically bled onto the page, nothing she said now would matter.

Evan's eyes widened slightly, then narrowed again. His posture stiffened. She could still read him. He remembered.

"You've got it wrong."

What? "Oh I do, huh? Then explain to me what I'm missing." Pain burned in her throat and she spat each one word like a dagger. "You told your buddy that he wouldn't want me because I was six kinds of crazy. All while you were draped all over a cheerleader and laughing at me behind my back. That about right?" She pulled away from him, her heart threatening to tear itself apart. "The man I left that night was someone who could never have truly cared about me."

Evan hung his head. "I didn't know you heard that."

Obviously. She wrapped her arms around her middle, determined to finish lancing this festering wound. "I drove up to campus that night. I'd wanted to come to surprise you. Spend a little time with you before I left for Atlanta. Instead I found out what you really thought of me."

He shook his head, locks of brown hair brushing his forehead. "That's not what I meant."

Ha. Back peddling. Trying to figure a way out of what he'd said. And here she'd thought maybe he'd grown up a little.

"Abs, you don't know Cal." He straightened, and the gentle man before her hardly resembled the cocky guy she used to know. He regarded her with a quiet confidence that contradicted his former swagger. "Cal was a grade A jerk. But he was also my teammate. My quarterback."

What did that have to do with anything?

Evan's face hardened. "He had his eye on you for

his next conquest." His gaze bored into her, and her insides constricted. "He asked me about you. I couldn't tell him to stay away from you without him seeing it as a challenge. I'd heard rumors about other girls and…" Disgust twisted his mouth into a snarl. "I couldn't risk him deciding he'd have you one way or another. So I said the only thing I could think of to deter him."

He'd…been trying to protect her? The only way he'd thought he could?

"You're not crazy, Abs. Why would you think I meant that?"

The heat drained from her, leaving her with a chill. She'd been wrong. So terribly wrong. But then…what if he was just finding anything he could say to get her to believe the lie? Like her father had for all those years?

How could she know?

He took her hand. "Why didn't you tell me you were there? We could have talked about it. I would have told you."

Abigail gently pried her fingers from his. "It doesn't matter now."

Evan flung his hand toward the papers in the hearth, his eyes saying what his lips didn't have to.

Fine. Yes. It mattered. Still hurt even though she'd fought to bury those emotions. He continued to stare at her until her frazzled composure ripped open and words burst out of her.

"My mother called me crazy. Did you know that?

Every time I wondered aloud or asked questions about things that didn't add up with my father, she'd get furious. Tell me I was crazy. Once, she accused me of being jealous." Things had never been the same after that. The more insecure Mom became, the more she took her pain out on Abigail with cutting words, snide retorts, and the complete withdrawal of affection. By the time her mother passed, they hadn't spoken in months.

Sadness cloaked Evan's voice. "Why didn't you tell me?"

Abigail shrugged. Who would want anyone knowing something like that? Even her best friend. She'd never told anyone about the problems she'd had with Mom. In many ways, she'd tried to pretend those problems, and her nagging doubts, didn't exist. With Dad gone most of the time, Mom was the one she had to appease. The relationship had fully fractured by the time Abigail left for college.

"I'm so sorry." Evan squeezed the bridge of his nose. "I was trying to protect you, not hurt you." He sighed. "So that's why you left? Why you wouldn't return my calls?"

She nodded.

"All that wasted time." Evan sighed, his words soft and laced with regret. "What exactly happened with your father? What truth did you discover that caused you to explode and get fired? Was it related to your problems with your mother?"

Abigail drew a shuddering breath. She hadn't told anyone—well, save all the people in Dad's office that day—but not anyone who mattered to her. The truth wormed through her middle, desperate to break free. To find release.

Evan's gentle eyes encouraged her to trust him. Did she dare? Probably not. Still, she couldn't hold onto this secret much longer.

Abigail drew a deep breath and released the ugly truth on a whisper. "My dad, he…" She hung her head. "We weren't his real family."

Eight

*T*his wasn't making sense. Evan ran his fingers across his chin. Maybe he hadn't heard Abigail correctly. "What do you mean, you weren't your dad's *real* family?"

"We were a…" She pulled her lower lip through her teeth. "A duplicate family. A sham. When we thought he was traveling, he was really home with his actual family. The first woman he married. The daughter he meant to have."

"So you're saying your mom was the mistress?"

She glared at him. "She *thought* she was his wife. They had a wedding."

How could a man marry two women? Wasn't that illegal? "I'm not following you, Abs."

"My father was already a married man when he met my mother. He had a one-year-old child. But he dated Mom, proposed to her, and pretended to marry her."

"How in the world do you pretend to marry someone?"

Abigail pushed the hair off her forehead and shivered. "It's cold and dark in here. Can we talk about this later?"

In the middle of her spilling a monumental secret? He understood this had to be difficult for Abigail, but she was notorious for avoiding uncomfortable conversations. This time, he wouldn't accept her excuse. "I'll build the fire."

Lips sealed tight, she waited while he gathered and stacked the wood by the hearth. Now that they'd started this whole mixed-up conversation, he wanted to understand.

"So how did he *pretend* to marry her?" Evan asked again.

Abigail sniffled. "I don't have all the details, exactly. All I know is they had a wedding. I've seen the pictures. He must not have filed for a license. At least, I never found one. Or any record of one, for that matter." She rubbed her temples. "When Mom passed, I started digging into things. I made a few discoveries that inflamed suspicions that had always nagged in the back of my mind—those ones that made Mom call me crazy. First, our house was in his name, but not hers. That got me thinking, but it wasn't exactly odd for a note to be in only one spouse's name. But then, so were the bank accounts. And every bill. All of it. Mom didn't have her name on *anything* they'd shared. In fact, until her death, I didn't realize she'd never legally changed her name to

Martin. There was no paperwork with her married name anywhere."

Evan stacked pieces of wood in the fireplace as he listened. He could use some tinder, but he wouldn't stop her to go find any. He poked at the embers, willing there to be enough life left in the coals to spark a flame. When the silence stretched, he met her gaze.

"I started asking myself questions," Abigail continued. "Why did he have a separate insurance policy for us? Why didn't mom have any accounts or assets of her own? The more I dug, the more wary I became. Even still, I figured he must have a logical explanation. When he offered for me to come work with him, I jumped at the chance." Guilt, mingled with disgust, crossed her face. "He gave me an apartment, a car, a credit card to buy all new clothes. He seemed so excited for me to be there.

"But when I started asking him questions, he said he wanted to look to the future, not relive the pain of the past. So I quit asking. Figured maybe it didn't matter. My parents' mess was their own."

Evan had never gotten to know Abigail's father in the way that she had known his family, but he couldn't fathom the logistics of David Martin living a double life. And for twenty-five years? How was it remotely possible he'd never been caught?

"Anyway, the truth finally came out when I met his wife."

Evan set the poker down and turned to face her. "Wait. You met his wife? The one he'd had since before your mom?" This story made less sense the longer Abigail talked. Why put the daughter he'd tried to hide in the middle of the life he'd kept secret from her? Wasn't that asking for trouble?

"He didn't know she was coming to the office that day. Or that I would be in the breakroom when she decided to drop off a cake for him." She crossed her arms. "Look, I know it sounds crazy, okay? But we started talking. She told me she was his wife. I asked her questions. Casually. Found out how long they'd been married. That they had a daughter, Amelia, three years older than me."

A small flame sprouted and licked at the wood. Evan adjusted one of the logs in hopes it would catch, then turned back to Abigail, choosing his words carefully. "So your dad had another family. One he never wanted you to find out about. But he invited you to come to Atlanta to work in his office…and what? Thought you'd never realize he was married to another woman?"

"I'm not an idiot, Evan."

What? He never said she was. And what did that have to do with her father's secret wife?

"She doesn't live in Atlanta. She lives two hours to the north, in the mountains. He goes home on the weekends. She never comes to the office."

Except on Mr. Martin's birthday, apparently. Talk about the proverbial tangled web. "Then how in the world did he have two families in two states and work in a different city than both of them?" Evan rocked back on his heels and stared at her in the faint light.

Abigail sat in the desk chair and rubbed her arms. "When I was a kid, he was a manager for his company...before he became CEO. Two weeks in Jackson, Mississippi, two weeks at the corporate office in Atlanta." Her words came out as cold as the winter air seeping around the window and leaking into the room.

Okay, yeah. He remembered that much from high school. Mr. Martin was home only on evenings and weekends a couple of weeks a month. Evan had never thought much of it. He'd always figured the guy traveled a lot.

"His wife bought a chateau in the Blue Ridge mountains after their daughter went to college. Said she loved it up there. They spend weekends together in the mountains. He keeps an apartment downtown during the week." Abigail shrugged. "Apparently that works for them."

She spoke as though she were telling him the morning's headline. Flat and emotionless. Which meant either she had separated herself from the hurt or had come to a place of understanding. He studied her. "Okay..." He drew the word out. "And none of your coworkers ever mentioned his wife or daughter? Did they know *you* were also his daughter? You have the same last name. How did you not hear about them all that time you worked there?"

Abigail glared at him. "I worked on a different floor. He said he wanted me to earn my place on my own merit, so I didn't mention our relationship to anyone. The younger people I worked with hardly knew anything about the higher-ups on the top floor. I wasn't even supposed to go up there, except it was his birthday, and I thought—"

She cut off, shaking her head. Evan filled in the pieces. If Mr. Martin really did have this double life, and had managed it for so long, maybe he'd gotten cocky. Thought a low-level employee he hardly crossed paths with wouldn't be noticed, even if they did share a last name. In a company that large, maybe no one thought anything about it. Maybe he'd given Abigail the job, car, and apartment out of guilt. And if any of the co-workers knew about those…they could have thought she was a young mistress. Maybe. Things like that happened. It could explain why no one would want to mention the CEO's wife around her.

Regardless, Abigail clearly felt foolish for having been so thoroughly deceived, so he wouldn't keep badgering her with questions to slake his own curiosity about how Mr. Martin had managed to keep such a secret. But he did want to know what had happened when she'd gotten fired and had been upset enough to call Evan's mom.

He kept his tone gentle. "So then what happened when, you know—"

"When I exploded, got fired, and my dad said he never wanted to see me again?" She barked out a bitter laugh. "Why does it matter?"

Evan rose and made a move toward her, but her slight recoil warned him now wasn't the time to try to comfort her. Instead, he settled back into his crouch and focused on the fire.

A flame caught a smaller log, and a warm glow started. Evan took a moment to blow on the coals and coax it to life. In another moment, he had a decent blaze.

The light danced across the room, illuminating Abigail's face. A face she kept indifferent. He sighed. Maybe she'd shared enough for one night. But the words she'd scrawled over the page kept nagging at him. Did she think that, because her father hadn't committed fully to her mother, *she* was somehow lacking? Not worthy of love?

"It's not your fault—what happened with your parents. You know that, right?"

Abigail's face remained flat. "Of course."

"It doesn't mean you weren't enough."

Her eyes sparked, shooting their own kind of fire in the flickering light.

He eased closer until he was kneeling in front of

her. "You are spunky and intuitive. You have a beautiful mind." He grabbed her fingers. "Abigail." He waited until she looked at him. "You are more than enough. You are everything."

Tears streaked down her face. Maybe he should hold his tongue. But he'd waited so long. Missed so many opportunities.

"You may not feel the same about me as I feel for you. That's okay. If you want to go back to being friends, like we used to be, then I'll be the best friend I can." He held her wavering gaze. "I'm not the jerk you used to know. God had a way of teaching me a little humility. All I ask is that you trust me enough to give me a chance to show you."

A small nod. Uncertain, but it was something. If he fought for her, could he build on their friendship and see if they uncovered something deeper?

Would she come to love him one day, even if she was uncertain now?

The possibility sparked an ember of hope that glowed more fiercely than the fledgling fire in the hearth. All he needed was a glimmer. He'd hold onto that for now. At the moment, she needed to know he wouldn't push her to reveal more than she was ready to. He could prove he would be here for her, no matter how long it took for her to trust him.

"I'm sorry your parents put you through that. Your father deceiving you. Your mother calling you crazy for having the intuition to realize something was off. That wasn't fair."

Abigail searched his face, as though wondering if he meant what he'd said. Finally, she squeaked out a small, "Thanks."

He squeezed her hand. They'd done enough unearthing for one day. "Let's get you tucked into bed. Maybe we can make sense out of this time warp thing in the morning."

"Or we'll wake up back at the inn, having discovered nothing," she huffed.

He didn't know about that. He'd certainly discovered more about Abigail than he'd bargained for. If they hadn't landed here, would she have ever told him the truth about her parents? Seemed to him Abigail had suspected her father's double life for some time. Judging by Mrs. Martin's reactions to Abigail's questions along those lines, maybe she had too—and hadn't wanted the truth discovered. Maybe Mrs. Martin knew all along. Or had found out but wanted to deny the truth at all costs—becoming angry if Abigail came too close to unearthing the secret. He'd probably never know.

His heart clenched. No wonder Evan calling her crazy had wounded her so deeply.

The line in Mrs. Easley's letter about discovering truths they hadn't been looking for surfaced in his brain.

His skin tingled. The woman couldn't have known, could she?

He tried for a grin but didn't think he accomplished much more than stretching his lips. "Waking up in our own time wouldn't be a bad thing. What are you hoping to find here?"

She made a sour face. "I *wanted* to know how the time travel worked."

Suddenly her reason for going to that inn made sense. If he had this many questions about her tangled past, he could only imagine what it must be like for her. Would he have taken a chance on an outlandish theory if he'd thought it might bring him answers? Possibly.

"I'm guessing it's not anything we can control, even if we do figure out how it works."

Disappointment flashed across her features and he wished there was something he could tell her to wipe it away. Maybe he should have listened more when all those Marvel fans discussed the different time warp theories.

"You're probably right." She rose quickly, seeming to draw her defenses around her once again. "Thanks for building the fire. Guess we better get some sleep."

Yeah. If they could. He eyed the door. "Want me to stay in here with you?"

She hesitated.

"I can sleep on the floor by the door."

A wry grin curved her lips. "How about I sleep by the fire, and you can have the bed?"

"Deal."

Had she lost her mind? Even in their years of teenage friendship, she and Evan had never shared a room. Abigail watched him fold quilts and place them by the fire. Close enough to keep warm, far enough away to be safe. She couldn't deny that his company brought comfort.

The words he'd spoken played on a loop in her head. *I'm sorry I never told you that I love you.*

Evan Blake loved her? The friend she'd once crushed on? The jock who'd been out of her league in college? The thoughtful, determined man before her?

Evan *had* changed. In the short time since she'd been thrust into his company again, she could tell. The bizarre circumstances brought out the differences more prominently.

You are more than enough. You are everything.

Did he really mean that? He turned to find her staring, and a slow smile spread over his unnervingly handsome face. The lines of his strong jaw. The spark in those gorgeous eyes. They were enough to make any girl's heart flounder.

As though reading her thoughts, the grin widened.

Yep. There was the cocky man she remembered. She put her hands on her hips. "You'll have to leave so I can get ready for bed."

Rather than a snarky remark that she could go right ahead with him here, which she'd expected, Evan gave a solemn nod. "Sure." Without another word, he strode from the room and closed the door with a soft click.

Changed for sure. Abigail sighed. She felt as wrung-out as a dishrag, her emotions dripping in puddles all around her. Evan said he loved her. He had been trying to protect her when he'd called her crazy. Now, he knew the truth about her messed up family.

She had no idea how to deal with all of that, and she was too tired to trust her brain to think clearly. After untying the stained apron and shimmying out of the dress, Abigail inspected the layers underneath she hadn't paid attention to earlier when she'd exchanged the fancy dress—and its weird petticoat thing that had given her ridiculously puffed-out hips—for the plain one.

She had on some kind of stiff and stifling corset thing that actually made her stand with great posture. Two bags hung tied around her waist, serving as hidden pockets. In both the fancy dress and the simpler one she'd worn to the basement, there had only been slits in the sides of the skirt so that she could access these pockets underneath. They were huge. She could probably hide all kinds of things under her dress if she needed to.

She untied the corset, and a long stick of wood fell out of the front. What in the world? No wonder she'd had such a hard time bending forward. Why did women want to shove a stick down the front of their dress?

After dropping the stick and the corset on the desk, she untied the pockets from around her waist and added them to the pile.

"Ready?" Evan's voice called from the hallway.

She grunted. "Not yet. There are way too many layers. Hold on."

Good grief. If she'd been cold with all this mess on, she could only imagine how much worse the winter would be without them. Two heavy wool underskirts hit the floor before she was finally left with thick, knee-high socks, clunky shoes, and a long white nightgown thing.

The shoes and socks she left by the desk. Convenient that these women wore their nightgowns under their clothes. Guess they didn't want to have to completely strip in the relentless cold.

Finally finished, she called to Evan. "You can come in now."

Evan opened the door carrying an armload of quilts he must have brought from his room. He gave her a once-over, appearing uncomfortable. "I thought you were going to get into your pallet."

She held out her arms. "That was before I knew I was wearing a grandma nightgown under my dress." Without a stitch of underwear, no less. But Evan didn't need to know that part. She waved a hand up him. "What about you. Do you need to change?"

"I'll sleep like this. In case anything happens and I

need to get up quickly."

To protect her. The unspoken meaning settled around her shoulders. She tried to swallow, but her tongue stuck to the roof of her mouth. Feeling oddly nervous, she hurried to her pallet and slipped under the first fold of the quilt, pulling it up to her chin.

Evan plopped the quilts on the bed settled on top of them, feet crossed at the ankles, shoes still on.

"You really think there will be trouble?" She'd wanted his company but hadn't considered that they might be in danger.

"Best to be cautious."

Silence settled on them, and Abigail stared into the flames. "Evan?" she asked softly.

"Yeah?"

You really love me? Like a friend or as more? The words stuck in her throat. "Good night."

"Good night."

She stared at his barely visible form in the gloom. "Evan?"

A smile lit his voice. "Yeah?"

"I'm glad you're here."

"I'm glad to be anywhere you are." A soft chuckle rumbled out of his chest. "Even if you did drag me through a wormhole."

Warmth that had nothing to do with the fire coiled in her middle. They settled into silence again.

"Abigail?"

"Yeah?"

"I'm sorry I didn't believe you. About the time-travel thing."

She laughed and snuggled deeper into her little nest. "That's okay. Not exactly the easiest theory to embrace."

"Still." He sighed. "I should have trusted you. I'm sorry."

Until that moment, she hadn't realized how desperately she'd wanted him to believe her. To trust her. Tears gathered in her eyes. In a matter of days, her entire world had shifted. Mostly for the bad.

She glanced at the bed. Except…Well, except for one glimmering possibility she couldn't begin to understand.

Nine

*M*orning sunlight washed over the small room and pulled Abigail from her sleep. She groaned and snuggled deeper into the covers. Warm. She shifted. Though her bed was a bit hard. This was the most uncomfortable bed she'd—wait. The previous day's events crashed onto her senses, chasing away the last sticky-eyed residue of sleep.

Time travel. The founding fathers. Spilled soup.

Evan.

She glanced at the bed but found only rumpled blankets. Abigail popped up, a heavy quilt falling from her shoulders. Worry flitted through her veins and tingled along her skin. "Evan?"

The door suddenly opened, and Evan strode through, his wide shoulders and toned arms obviously unstrained by the burden of wood he carried for the fire. "Morning. We're still here." He closed the door with his foot.

She couldn't stop the warm feeling that bloomed in

her middle. Still *here*, here where Evan had said he *loved her*. She'd stayed awake most of the short night thinking about those words.

Grabbing the top quilt and keeping it around her shoulders, Abigail stepped off her pallet to give Evan access to the fireplace. Awkwardness flooded her chest. Things could never be the same between them. Not now. Now that she'd spilled the ugly truth about her family and the mess of her life.

The past seemed to have a way of overtaking everything these days.

"Sleep well?" Evan asked, studying her.

Her cheeks heated under his narrowed gaze. Did he regret what he'd said? Abigail pulled the quilt tighter around her shoulders and offered a timid smile. "Uh, yeah. I guess." Why would she feel so flustered around Evan? A man she'd known since he was a gangly fourteen-year-old with knobby knees?

Because he'd said he loved her. And she didn't know what to do with that.

He stacked the pile of firewood by the hearth. The flames inside still glowed cheerfully, and surprisingly the room felt decently warm. Shouldn't the fire have died down in the night? Yawning, she stretched her arms over her head. They'd probably gone to bed super late. Without clocks, her sense of time was out of whack.

"They have coffee downstairs," Evan said as he dropped on another log.

Thank goodness. A girl needed a little caffeine to start a day of colonial patriotism. The weird feeling dissipated, and she latched onto the comfort of simple conversation. "Any good?"

"Decent." He chuckled. "Don't ask for tea, though."

Right. The whole tea tax thing. Abigail chuckled. "Gotcha."

Evan brushed his hands down pants that clung to his muscular legs. A strange sensation sparked in her stomach, and she looked away. "Thanks again for the fire."

"Sure." He shuffled his buckled shoes. "They have breakfast. Want to go eat?"

The mention of food awakened her stomach, and it growled in response.

Evan raised a brow, causing her to chuckle.

"Yeah. I'm starving. I don't think I've eaten since before I got on the plane, and that feels like a year ago."

She didn't remember all that much from history class, but she knew that a hot shower and a hair dryer were impossibilities. Ugh. How long would they have to go without bathing? She wrinkled her nose at the thought.

"You just thought about the bathroom thing." Evan laughed. "Didn't you?"

Abigail eyed him. "So you've been to the 'privy' too?"

He trembled in an exaggerated shudder. "Another reason to not hang around in the eighteenth century. No wonder these people smell so bad."

The unfamiliar scents had been so overwhelming that Abigail hadn't been able to identify the sources of the offending odors. She stifled a groan. She'd had to use the stinky little outhouse right before she'd started helping Mrs. Hugley serve supper last night. And hadn't returned. She wouldn't be able to avoid a trip much longer.

First, she'd need to get dressed. She eyed the pile of clothing on the desk. Mercy. How would she ever get the mass of layers back on? As much as her insides twisted at asking, she did need help. And there was no one else. "Do you think you can…uh…help me with all this stuff? I don't know if I'll ever get all the ties done up on my own. Or if I do it'll take forever."

He blinked as though she'd just asked him to solve a physics equation. Then his Adam's apple bobbed. Yep, she could relate. Totally weird to ask someone to help you get dressed. Especially after last night.

Probably a bad idea. She could figure something out. "That's okay. I can—"

"Tell me what you need." He stepped closer, shoving his hands in the pockets of his long jacket.

Abigail surveyed the stack. Did she really need that corset? The past hadn't given her any undergarments, and the stiff corset had been worn over the top of this nightgown thing. Maybe it was necessary for the proper fit of the dress. And another layer—however uncomfortable—would be more armor against the relentless cold.

That poofy hip enhancer thing, though, she was definitely going without. Who in the world wanted to walk around looking like she had two pillows sticking to the sides of her thighs? These people had weird ideas about fashion.

She grabbed the corset and wrapped it around her waist. "Here. Pull this tight and tie it."

Evan made a weird little noise but grabbed the strings and pulled. He fumbled a moment, and the corset cinched her torso. He stepped back. "There. Done."

Next Abigail pulled both wool underskirts over her head. Those she tied without issue, and the baggy pockets were simple enough to fasten around her waist. Maybe she could handle this after all.

"That's a lot of layers."

"Yep," she said as her fingers pulled the strings tight.

"What's that thing?" Evan pointed to the flat stick on the table.

"No clue. It came out of the front of this corset thing, but I don't know what it's supposed to be." She stepped around him and pulled open the wardrobe. "This is the hard part."

Inside, several dresses hung from pegs and wooden hangers. Yesterday's gown of golden fabric with a red and green flower pattern had been pretty, but she'd nearly frozen. Best find something more suited to wandering around outside, as she was sure Evan would want to do. She chose one that looked like a thick wool in a soft dove gray. Hopefully it would be the warmest. "Help me get this thing on."

"Why do women wear all that stuff when men are supposed to go around in stockings and tights?" Evan grumbled.

"Maybe you're more suited to the cold." A nervous chuckle bubbled out of her. Ugh. She sounded like a giggling thirteen-year-old with a crush. She clamped her lips tight.

Together they got the folds of the gown over Abigail's head and settled across all the other pieces. Evan tugged and twisted until they finally had the gown situated.

Her nerves skittered. No one had helped her dress since she'd been six years old. Having Evan do so felt strangely intimate. Her cheeks heated, and she stepped away from his touch. "Come on. I want to get to breakfast."

"I think you have to put your hair up," Evan said. "Maybe even wear one of those little cap things."

Oh right. Abigail nodded. She hadn't seen even one woman with her hair down. Good thing she still had a hair elastic. She twisted the length of her thick brown hair into a messy bun and wrapped the elastic around the wad. "There. Let's go."

He grinned. "You look great."

In this costume with no makeup and no chance to brush her teeth? Hardly. But then, Evan had never looked at her like that before. Almost like she was the Heisman trophy.

Something warm she dared not identify swam in his eyes, and her breath caught.

"Uh, thanks." She darted out the door before he could say anything else. She was a mess already, and she didn't need him flirting with her like she was some cheerleader at a party.

Evan followed her downstairs and waited near the back door while she ran out to do her business. A few frigid, stinky, and undeniably unpleasant moments later, she returned.

"Winter. Why Boston in the winter?"

"It's not *that* cold." Evan chuckled. "And you're wearing a hundred layers of wool."

She huffed. "Still cold." Wool or not, this weather chilled to the bone.

"You weren't built to be a snow bunny, that's for sure." Evan chuckled again, clearly enjoying her misery. She smacked playfully at his arm, but that only made him laugh more.

They made their way into a dining room much more

subdued than last night's lively gathering. A few women added splashes of femininity to the tables, but for the most part the room remained undeniably masculine.

Not even the decor held a touch of womanly design. Huh. Come to think of it, shouldn't there be Christmas decorations everywhere?

They'd landed here on December fourteenth, and there was not a wreath or string of garland in sight. Abigail found the notion odd. People back home barely took down Halloween decorations before stringing up Christmas lights.

She and Evan took seats at a wood plank table, and a girl bustled over. Probably no more than fourteen or fifteen, if Abigail had to guess. Shouldn't she be in school?

"Breakfast for you and the missus, sir?"

Evan made a garbling sound but quickly cleared his throat to cover. "Yes. Thank you."

Abigail cocked an eyebrow but left the *missus* thing alone. Best find something safe to talk about. "Did you notice there are no Christmas decorations? Colonials are staunch Puritans, right? Wouldn't they celebrate Christmas?"

Seeming relieved at the mundane topic of conversation, Evan said, "I think in the old days people put up Christmas decorations on Christmas Eve. Then they celebrated the twelve nights of Christmas, with parties and such on January sixth."

"Where did you learn that?"

"Saw a Christmas special on George Washington."

When had Evan started watching documentaries?

"No Christmas decorations is fine by me. I hate the idea of Christmas this year anyway."

He lifted an eyebrow in question.

Why had she said that? She opened her mouth to downplay the statement with some kind of joke, but the truth tumbled out instead. "Just not feeling all that festive this year, I guess. Knowing about my family kind of soured my idea of what the holiday should be."

"Sorry, Abs."

She sighed. "It stinks realizing so much of your life was a lie. Now I know that the years we'd had to celebrate Christmas on different days wasn't because of Dad's work schedule. Those must have been years he spent Christmas day with his other wife and daughter." She shook her head. "I wonder how he decided which family he wanted."

The young waitress returned with two bowls of something that looked like runny grits and a hunk of hard cheese.

"I just don't get it," Abigail said as the girl walked off. "Why live a lie that complicated? That…devious?"

"I don't know." Evan stuck his spoon into his bowl and let the mush slide back off. "The whole thing sounds a bit—uh." He pressed his lips together to stop the word she already knew he'd meant to say.

"Crazy? I know. Believe me. I know." She sampled the hard cheese, but it tasted sour.

Evan took a bite of the mush and grimaced. "Not exactly what I'd been hoping for."

At least there was coffee. Bitter coffee that needed a lot of cream, but caffeine was caffeine.

"Yeah." Abigail spooned a tiny bite and stuck it between her lips. "Tastes like nothing, really. Too bad we don't have any salt and pepper. That would probably help."

They ate the mush in silence, filling their stomachs more than enjoying a meal. Finished, Abigail pushed the bowl away.

Evan pushed away his own bowl and looked around the room. "How do we get the check?"

"Haven't seen one delivered to anyone, so I guess it comes with the room."

"And we pay for that how?"

"Beats me."

Evan rose and offered his hand with a mischievous flourish. "So, my lady, what shall we do on this fine eighteenth-century morning?"

She couldn't help but smile at his new acceptance of their bizarre trip. "I don't know. What do you think we should do?"

He grinned. "A tour? Followed by lunch somewhere else? Maybe a look at the docks?"

The entire day strolling around with Evan. Like…a

date? Butterflies fluttered in her stomach. She slid her fingers into his. "Sounds good."

The spark of hope Evan had felt last night burst into flame. Abigail stood staring up at him with something new shining in her eyes. Had all their conversations given them some kind of breakthrough?

He felt as though they were rolling downhill and gaining speed—something that he figured would have terrified him and yet…it didn't.

Hand in hand, they strolled out into a sunny but chilly morning. Sometime during the night a light dusting of snow must have fallen. It clung to the edges of windows and sprinkled rooftops in shimmering white.

Abigail paused. "Too bad snow has to be so cold. Otherwise it would be nice to look at."

Evan chuckled at the wry humor in her tone. Maybe it was a good thing he hadn't been drafted. What if he'd ended up in Green Bay or somewhere equally as cold? Abigail wouldn't have survived.

"Pretty snow or not, it doesn't make up for the stench." Abigail put her fingers under her nose.

Like yesterday, horses, carts and people clogged the streets of Boston. The smells, even in the fresh air, were rank. Livestock, sea brine, body odor, sewage, and who knew what else clogged his nostrils.

"The past sure is smelly," Abigail said.

Evan paused and looked both ways. "Extremely. Which way do you want to go?"

"You pick."

Interesting. Abigail usually had an opinion on everything. He steered them toward the harbor. "I'd like to see these ships Adams was carrying on about last night."

"Oh!" Abigail's grip tightened on his arm. "I completely forgot to ask you about the meeting. What did you learn?"

They paused for a man driving a massive hog down the road with a stick.

When the man and hog had passed, Evan said, "Not much, really. They talked about the taxes and refusing to let the ships unload. Well, they can unload other cargo, just not the tea. Honestly, I don't think there's much to learn since we already know that they're about to dress like a bunch of Indians and dump all that tea into the harbor."

They passed several shops where men or boys swept away snow. Occasionally, someone called out wares to people passing.

"I don't get it," Abigail said. "Why did we end up *here*? Maybe we hit a glitch."

Evan studied the side of her smooth cheek. "You suspected you could time-travel and you *chose* to go to that house. Seems risky. Why do it?" He'd figured it was so she could see what happened with her parents, but instead of assuming, he'd rather she tell him.

They continued down the street at a leisurely stroll. Abigail remained quiet for half a block. Maybe she didn't plan to answer him.

"I wasn't really thinking clearly," Abigail finally said, sounding a little exasperated. "I wanted a miracle. Not a trip to…Boston." She waved a hand to indicate all that one word entailed.

She'd wanted a miracle. Like her friend Maddie. He no longer thought she was looking for a husband to take home. At least, he didn't think so. "Were you trying to go back to the beginning?" he prompted. "To the start of your parents' marriage and find out the truth?"

She huffed. "Sounds stupid. I know."

"Not stupid. You've been fed so many lies, you were looking for an opportunity to see how it all happened. That's natural."

Halting, Abigail stared up at him, beautiful eyes glassy. "You really think so?"

That slight quiver in her bottom lip captured his attention. Mesmerizing. He ran a thumb down her cheek. "Of course," he breathed. "Anyone would want to know."

She studied him a long moment, doing crazy things inside him. "Thanks." She turned on her heels and started down the street.

So much for the moment he'd thought they were having. Women. He'd never understand them. Evan kept pace with her and tried to focus on their surroundings. Anything to get the tightness in his chest to loosen and distract his thoughts from the overwhelming desire to sweep Abigail into his arms and kiss away all her worries.

What had gotten into him?

The tall masts of the ships rose above the roofs of a row of shops, so they turned that direction.

"Of course," Abigail said, picking up the conversation again as though she had no idea what she'd done to him, "I thought when Maddie said she'd found her greatest wish at The Depot, she meant something a little different." Her eyebrows dipped low, and she nibbled on her lower lip in that way she always did when she was upset.

"Like what?"

Abigail shrugged. "I don't know. I thought I could make a request."

"Like rubbing a lamp and getting three wishes from a genie?" He smirked, and the sparkle returned to her eyes.

Abigail laughed and lightly punched his arm. "You're a piece of work." But her grin softened the jab. "Stupid as that sounds, yeah. I guess I thought Maddie had asked to go back in time and pick up a man." She shook her head. "After everything that happened, I was feeling a little desperate. Pair that with having nowhere to go for Thanksgiving and…" She let the sentence dangle and shrugged, the shoulders of her wool dress hitching up toward her red ears.

"You had my—"

She held up a hand to stop his protest. "With nowhere to go except to be analyzed by your sister, asked a million questions by your parents, and face…" She cut him a look.

His stomach clenched. Face *him*. The guy she'd thought had shamed her in front of his friends. He gave a knowing nod. "Say what you want, but you called my mom, not an Uber to take you to a B&B from the airport. Ask me, I think you were looking for an invite home. Even if you planned to refuse it."

Color flooded her cheeks. Yep. That assumption sailed straight through the uprights. Point, Evan.

Abigail ignored his insight and continued as though he hadn't just uncovered the truth. "I thought I could make a request to see what happened with my dad." She barked a humorless laugh. "Though I honestly don't know what good I thought that would do. Knowing doesn't change anything."

"The truth can bring peace. Set you free." He knew. But now wasn't the time for sharing how deeply he understood.

"I guess. Except I didn't get any answers and instead got you stuck in the 1700s."

He bumped her shoulder. "I don't mind being stuck here with you."

Those brilliant eyes glimmered, and her expression shifted. "You really mean that?"

Of course he did. Why did she continually question everything he said? Would he ever be someone people believed? He tried to push the hurt aside and remember she'd been lied to. Reassurance was understandable, even if her need for it from him grated. He put as much sincerity into his words as he could. "More than you know."

The muscles in her neck tightened as she swallowed hard. "I'm glad I'm not here alone."

The warmth went out of him. He held in a scoff. She wasn't glad *he* was here with her. Anybody would've done, so long as she hadn't gotten stuck in this awful place by herself. And here he'd thought there was something blooming between them.

When would he ever learn? Evan cleared his tight throat and pointed toward the ships. "How about we take a look at the boats?"

An expression he couldn't quite understand passed over her face. Confusion? Annoyance? She smoothed her features quickly and lifted her chin.

"Right. Find out what we have to so we can get home." Abigail strode off.

Leaving him to scramble after her. Yep. Women. He'd never understand them.

Men. They didn't understand anything. Abigail marched down the street, heading toward the massive ships. She'd thought they were having a moment. She'd opened herself up, let him know she was glad he was with her. And he hadn't even responded.

Except…Well, maybe that wasn't exactly what she'd said. She'd said she was glad she wasn't alone. Groaning, she slowed her steps.

Evan gained her side with a stony expression, gazing at the ships. "They sure are big. I guess I never thought about how much tea a ship like that would carry."

Abigail touched his arm. "I'm sorry."

He dropped his gaze to search her face. The cold wind played with his hair, swirling it over his arched eyebrows. "For?"

No letting her off easy. "For making it seem like I wasn't glad *you* are here with me." She shifted, hating herself for feeling awkward. But he'd changed everything between them, and that made for uneven footing. "I'm trying to say I'm glad you insisted on going to the inn. I'm happy you came here with me. Glad you said, uh…" She stepped closer and looked up into his eyes, searching. "Those things you said. Did you really…I mean, you were talking about as friends, right? Not as—"

Her words cut off as Evan's lips suddenly landed on

hers. Her breath caught. Evan Blake was *kissing* her. Neurons fired in her brain, and her senses kicked in. He was kissing her, and if she didn't respond, he'd stop. Abigail returned the gentle pressure of his mouth. Breathed him in.

His lips were soft. Strong, yet gentle. Everything and more she'd once imagined they would be. Heart thudding, she stepped closer and grabbed his lapels, a sense of rightness, longing, and warmth spreading through her, muddling her thoughts and setting her nerves on fire.

The people on the street, the cold, the ships in the harbor, 1773... Nothing mattered except the over-whelming sense of perfection that came from melting into Evan's arms. He pulled her closer against him, his warmth enveloping her.

He suddenly pulled back, breaking a connection that had pulled her under a current she might never have surfaced from again. Maybe she wouldn't want to. Of course she wouldn't. Why would she need to breathe when the alternative felt so much better? She stared at him, every inch of her tingling.

That slow, confident grin lifted lips she already missed. "Wow."

Wow. Yeah. Abigail opened her mouth, but nothing came out. She swallowed and tried again. "So, maybe not as friends?"

He tilted his head back and roared a laugh. What?

How was that funny?

"Abs, you make it hard on a man, you know that?"

She started to pull away, but Evan held her firm. "I'm not sure how I'm bungling this, but let me try again. Abigail Martin. I love you. Yes, as my friend, but also as so much more. You make me want to be everything you need. I want to protect you, cherish you, and yes"—his eyes sparkled—"kiss you. As often as you'll let me."

Oh wow.

Her heart hammered, opening up a place inside she'd long buried. A place that reminded her that she'd wanted Evan to love her since she'd first met him. But he'd always had eyes for popular girls. For cheerleaders, for...

How many other girls had Evan said those same words to? How many others before her had he loved? A chill started in her center, forcibly pushing out the delicious tingles of warmth. Evan had dated more girls than Abigail could count. He'd never been anywhere without some pretty thing on his arm.

Abigail took a step back, the cold realization knifing through her. This wouldn't end well. Evan was a passionate guy. Once the newness wore off, wouldn't he be looking for the next girl? He'd never cheated on anyone, not that she knew of. But once his eye snagged on another female who caught his fancy, he'd drop the one on his arm in favor of the chase.

And her heart couldn't take being another girl left mooning after Evan Blake. She shook her head. "We…we shouldn't."

Pain gathered in his eyes, but she couldn't let herself fall down this rabbit hole. Evan might be a wonderland, but in the end she'd end up beheaded by another Queen of Hearts.

He reached for her, but she took another step back. "Maybe we should go back to the tavern."

Confusion drew his eyebrows low. Evan had probably never kissed a girl who didn't immediately turn into putty and throw her heart at his feet. The fact that she wanted to do exactly that terrified her.

"If I overstepped, I—"

"No." She sighed. "But I don't think we should, you know? Why mess up a friendship?"

"You mean the one where you don't answer my calls and try to avoid me at all costs?"

The mixture of dark humor and pain in his voice sliced her. "I'm sorry about that. If you'll forgive me for my assumptions and for not asking you about what happened, then maybe… Can we go back to how things were? You know, before?"

Evan looked at her like he was trying to analyze her in the same way his sister might. Abigail stood her ground, chin high.

"If that's what you want." His eyes darkened, and he stepped close again, his expression saying he could see that every fiber of her longed for more. "Are you *sure* that's all you want? Friendship?"

With the way he was looking at her now? No. A million times no. She wanted to pick out a white dress and a church and—

No. Those kinds of thoughts would only lead to a broken heart and the complete loss of the only family she had left.

But…what if it didn't? What if Evan loved her forever and his family really did become hers?

Or what if, after a few months, he got the one he thought he couldn't have out of his system and found someone new? Then she'd have no one.

"I just…can't."

He nodded and turned back the way they'd come, face unreadable. An overwhelming sense of loss clenched in her middle.

She'd made the right choice. If it hurt this bad to lose Evan after one kiss, she would have never survived the inevitable breakup later.

Ten

She'd lied to him. Evan could clearly see—no, feel—that Abigail wanted him. She'd been surprised at first by his spontaneous kiss, sure. But there'd been *nothing* in her returned kiss that hinted she thought of him like a friend.

Definitely not as a brother.

People on the street stared openly at them, many whispering to one another. Let them stare. Stuffy Puritans. He didn't care if kissing Abigail in public brought waves of gossip. He didn't care about much of anything at the moment except Abigail herself.

And the way her rejection was ripping him apart.

He'd kissed his share of women, but none had ever done crazy things to his insides like Abigail. There'd been such a sense of rightness at having her in his arms. The ache of loss now brought a chill that made the Boston winter feel like Hawaii.

What held her back? She wanted him, but she didn't want to be *with* him. "Abs, can we talk about—"

"Not now."

Anger stirred at the bite in her tone. Not talking about what he'd done to upset her the last time had cost him months of heartache. Communication mattered. The truth *mattered*.

Lord, You said patience, but this woman is testing every ounce I've got.

"Fine. But we *need* to talk. I don't want to pretend nothing happened."

She walked faster. Evan lengthened his stride, easily keeping pace. Did she think to run away from him? Not this time. She could be mad at him if she wanted, but she'd be mad with him at her side.

He wouldn't let her avoid him. Not again.

"Abigail. We need to—"

"Talk about it. I know." She suddenly came to a stop. "But there's nothing to say. Let's just leave it alone, okay?"

Her words thrust a knife into him and twisted. He kept his voice as even as he could. "Leaving your feelings unsaid too long only makes the situation worse." He shoved his hands into his pockets. Patience was becoming a real pain.

She drew a deep breath and released it in a puff of vapor. "Fine. You want to do this now?"

He gave a curt nod, steeling himself for however she planned to slice him.

"This is slippery ground," she said slowly, voice

uncertain. Then her face hardened as though she'd resolved her own internal debate. "I'm not one of those girls you pick up at parties. When this thing goes south, I lose an entire family." Her eyes shimmered, and the hardness fell away. "The only shadow of one I have left."

She thought…? Oh man. Of course she would. His chest constricted. Words wouldn't form. Abigail had seen him date lots of girls. But hadn't she also seen that he'd never really been serious with any of them? He'd date a girl, realize she wasn't what he was looking for, and move on. What was wrong with that? He never dated more than one girl at a time, and he'd always been up front when he didn't see a future.

Dating all those girls had showed him exactly who he didn't want…and who he did.

"You aren't someone I found attractive and then wanted to get to know, only to discover we weren't compatible." How could he explain? "You are the girl I called when I needed to sort out my thoughts. You're the one person I could talk to for hours and the only person I never get tired of."

Didn't she understand the difference? Loving the woman who had been his best friend was nothing like going on dates to get to know people.

Her eyes shimmered for at least the third time that morning. Man. He totally stank at this sharing emotions thing. Abigail offered a sad smile and started walking again.

What? No response? He laid his heart out for her, and she just walked away?

Patience.

Evan ground his teeth and followed. Patience. How could a man have patience when the woman he loved rejected every offer of his heart? Did nothing he said matter?

He couldn't promise everything would work out— as much as he wanted it to. He would put in the work for their relationship, but what if he gave everything he had, and in the end she decided he wasn't good enough for her?

Evan grunted. "Maybe you have a point." If things didn't work out, they wouldn't be able to go back to the way things used to be.

Expression unreadable, Abigail nodded. "I suppose we don't have anything to do now besides try to figure out a way to get home."

Home. The word jarred his memory. "Oh no. Adams wanted me to meet him and the others. I forgot all about it."

"When are you supposed to meet them? For supper in the basement again?" Her voice held a weariness he couldn't quite understand.

"Noon. Somewhere called the Liberty Tree." He tugged at the ruffles hanging at his throat. Worst tie ever. "They asked me about coming last night. I'm not sure what good listening to them will—"

"So what do *I* do while you go to a meeting?" She crossed her arms.

What? How had he made her mad now? Evan clenched his fists, all hope of keeping his patience with her vanishing.

She didn't want to walk with him, didn't want to discuss their relationship, and apparently didn't want him to go talk with those men. So what *did* she want from him?

There seemed to be no right answers here. Telling her she could do whatever she wanted felt like a play call that would get him tackled in a blitz defense. He almost said it anyway, but instead ground out, "Go with me?"

She gave him a flat look. "Somehow I doubt women are allowed to do anything more than serve the men. Clearly, I won't be asked to do that again."

"Should I not go?"

"You can go if you want to."

The words sprang like a trap. He glared at her. Was she being impossible on purpose? "We agreed that learning something for Mrs. Easley would be how we got home, so I think it's important to go. But I don't want to leave you either, so I think you should go with me."

Her eyes narrowed. Just what he'd thought. A question with no right answer.

"Okay."

Okay? Huh. He offered his arm as he'd seen other

men in this time do. Abigail gave him a funny look, but slipped her arm through his. Landmines averted.

Unless he'd misread her agreement and another trap would blindside him at any moment.

He looked up at the sky. The sun seemed nearly directly overhead. So, close to noon? He hadn't thought to ask where to find the other meeting place. He'd need to ask directions.

Abigail launched into a series of rapid-fire questions as they started down the street. "Are they still meeting about the tea? What does that have to do with Mrs. Easley? If she's trying to find out something that's not in the history books, then why not come here herself? It doesn't make any sense."

Whoa. "Not sure what any of it has to do with Mrs. Easley, but who knows what that woman was planning? The letter said we had to find answers. I'm pretty sure the men are still talking about the tea, the taxes, and the ships. Which we know they'll do until they decide to dump the shipment into the harbor."

As far as why the strange woman who had been dressed in a 1700s outfit hadn't come here herself, he had no answer for that. Maybe Mrs. Easley had planned on coming with them but something had happened to stop her.

"The letter said the answers we found wouldn't be the ones we sought."

Evan shook his head to clear his thoughts. Too

many questions. What answers did they seek? Easy. How to get home. Which looped them back to the letter and what they had to find out in order to get Mrs. Easley to time-warp them back to the present. "So we're back to square one?"

The questions were starting to make his head hurt.

"I don't know." Abigail sighed. "But I'm not sure listening to Samuel Adams is going to get us anywhere."

He hated not having a game plan. "Okay. If we aren't looking for answers in history, then I don't have a clue what we're supposed to find in order to get home."

Abigail didn't reply.

"What else did the letter say?" he mused out loud. "Something about a treasure? Are we looking for a pirate chest or something?"

He meant it as a joke to lighten the mood, but Abigail didn't laugh. "She said at the end we would discover a great treasure. Not that we would necessarily be looking for one. I don't know what treasure she means, but I doubt it's a pirate chest."

Evan grunted. He'd never liked puzzles. He wasn't the kind of guy who considered being locked in an escape room a fun evening out. Why couldn't the woman have been clear?

"Where is this tree you're supposed to find?" Abigail asked.

"The Liberty Tree. It's another tavern, from what I figured. These people talk so strangely."

"They probably think that about us."

Most likely.

Abigail tugged his arm. "Oh! We'll ask Mr. Barnard. He's over there."

She darted across the street, lifting her skirt and ducking between a boy leading a donkey and a man with a handcart. Muttering under his breath, Evan hurried after her.

The constable, the one who had asked Abigail if she needed to be relieved of Evan's company, turned sharp eyes on Evan as soon as he approached.

"How fortuitous. I was just sending men to fetch you, Mr. Blake."

"Fetch me?" Evan repeated.

"Why?" Abigail scrunched her nose.

The stout man nodded to two men beside him, both dressed in long coats and wearing triangular hats. The two men grabbed Evan's arms.

What in the world? "What are you doing? Let go of me." He didn't want to cause a commotion in unfamiliar territory, but he wouldn't be manhandled by men half a foot and fifty pounds smaller than he was, either.

"Wait," Abigail said. "There has to be some misunderstanding."

The pleading look she shot him was the only thing that kept him from dropping both men to the dirt.

The constable sneered at him. "No misunderstanding. I've had several reports this morning, all for a man matching Mr. Blake's unique description." He lifted his chin and spoke with finality. "For lewd and unseemly behavior, you are hereby sentenced to two hours in the stocks. Consider this a warning, Mr. Blake. We do not tolerate such wantonness here."

Lewd and unseemly? "What are you talking about?"

"You were seen in a most disturbing and disruptive public embrace by a multitude of witnesses." He cast Abigail a disgusted look. "Were you not?"

"I kissed her, yeah," Evan said. "There's nothing lewd about that."

The man grunted as though Evan had admitted to a crime and nodded to the men holding his arms. "Take him."

Evan snatched one arm free and pulled his fist back, but before he could release a punch the other man shoved the skinny barrel of a long pistol into his side.

He stilled, and they regained his arms, keeping the weapon close to his ribs.

"No." Abigail shouted, reaching to grab the constable. "I'm not pressing charges or anything. I didn't mind. Really. Evan did nothing wrong."

Francis ignored her. She continued to argue with him anyway, promising again that Evan hadn't done anything wrong. But the more she defended him, the more disgusted the constable looked. Would he lock her up as well?

"Abigail," Evan called over his shoulder as the men

hauled him away. "Don't. I'll be fine."

Her face paled, and he caught a look of terror in her eyes before the man with the gun jabbed him. "Keep moving."

"Sentencing without a trial?" Evan sneered. "Don't you people have laws and proper procedures?"

Neither man answered him.

He should probably keep his mouth shut before one of them shot him.

They came to the end of the street and entered what appeared to be a town square. In the center, three sets of stocks, the kind he'd seen in movies, stood on a raised platform.

Evan snorted and pulled back against his captors. "This is ridiculous."

The man at his right, a thin fellow with a pointy noise, leaned close. "Best you take your lumps, aye? Two hours isn't worth finding yourself in the correction house."

Correction house? That didn't sound good. Evan stopped struggling and allowed the men to bend his head toward the open stocks. The bottom piece of wood was carved with one large semicircle and two smaller ones. They pushed his neck into the larger hole and placed his wrists on each smaller one.

The top bar came down with a bang, and Evan winced. They locked him in place and strode away without a word. People on the street ignored him as though his predicament were nothing unusual. The rack was too tall for Evan to get on his knees, but too high for him to stand any way except in an uncomfortable bent position.

The stocks. For kissing a girl. They hadn't even given him a trial or hearing. How could they pull a guy off the street and stick him in a torture device without proper processing? Evan ground his teeth, his frustration growing.

Of all the stupid things!

Abigail hurried down the street, her pale cheeks splotchy red. "Evan!" She stopped in front of him, and he had to press the back of his head against the stocks to see her face.

"Oh, Evan. I'm sorry! I tried to stop him. But then he started saying I should be whipped and—"

"He what?" When he got out of this thing, he should give that guy a taste of his own vigilante justice.

"Can you believe that?" Abigail plopped down on the raised platform next to him and crossed her arms. Her indignation on his behalf calmed some of his ire. She had no clue how appealing she looked right now. "Of all the nerve." Abigail wagged her head. "What on earth is wrong with these people?"

Despite his situation, Evan chuckled. "Next time, we stay in our own century."

"Agreed." Abigail scooted closer. "I'm sorry I got us into this."

The contrition in her voice dissolved the remainder of his anger.

He grunted. "That's okay." It was difficult to stay mad at her when she looked at him like that.

"It's not, but thanks. Not to mention I've been a pill to deal with today."

He left that statement alone.

She leaned her back against the post. "This day sure hasn't turned out as we planned."

An understatement. Dark humor bubbled though him. "Since I'd planned on asking you out on a date and going to dinner and maybe a movie..." He barked a bitter laugh at the impossibly ludicrous shift in circumstances. "No, this weekend isn't at all what I planned." He'd cashed in all of his days off at the car dealership in hopes of spending the holiday with her.

No, nothing had gone at all like he'd first thought when he'd convinced his mom to let him pick Abigail up from the airport.

Abigail remained silent. They sat there for a time, watching people mill around the streets. As long as she planned on sitting here next to him, they might as well get everything out in the open. If his relationship with Abigail was going up in flames, then he at least wanted to say he'd held nothing back. Then he could move on without regrets.

"Since we're stuck here for a couple of hours, how about we dive into that tough conversation you want to avoid?"

Another of his attempts at humor to lighten the gravity of the topic fell flat. Abigail kept her focus on the streets. "You really want to do that now?"

Might as well. "I get your fears, Abs. But what if we miss out on something amazing?"

She crossed her arms and shivered. "You're not exactly the commitment type." She sighed. "I can't be another one of your ex-girlfriends. I'm sure they all thought they were someone special to you."

Her words sliced through him. Obviously she hadn't believed anything he'd said. "So you've made up your mind and won't even give me a chance to prove that you're wrong?"

Tears trickled down her cheeks. "I wish I could."

Anger scorched up his chest, and all thoughts of patience incinerated. "I guess you're right. We *are* doomed. Because I could never marry a woman who refuses to trust me."

Eleven

Shock flared through Abigail's center. *Marry*? Evan thought of *marrying* her? Or was that more of an expression? She stared at the top of his dark hair.

He hung his head, breaths puffing out like white smoke.

Should she stay here or give him some space? Talk about what he'd said or pretend the words had never left his lips? Tightness in her chest brought an ache she didn't expect. The pain at having lost Evan when she'd never known he could care for her that way put her heart through a press. Tears leaked out of her eyes and left cold tracks down her face.

"I want to believe you. I promise. It's just…I'm scared." She scooted a little closer to where he stood.

"You don't understand." His voice was calm. Almost dismissive. Somehow that hurt worse than if he'd yelled at her. "Trust is important."

She knew that better than anyone. She had trusted her father. Where had that gotten her? Neck-deep in lies and broken promises.

Evan shifted, and his voice gained strength. Laced with a steel she didn't recognize, yet it was still steady and direct. "You don't want to date me? Fine. But tossing me away without a thought because you can't believe what I told you? That cuts. Deeply."

He spoke softly, slowly. Each word opened a new wound in her already bleeding emotions. He was right.

The man before her had matured into someone steady and firm. Someone confident enough to speak his emotions clearly and directly. The man hanging here next to her in a humiliating position was nonetheless a tower of self-possessed strength, and her heart ached all the more for it. He was no longer the cocky teen she'd known or the egotistical football star. Those boys she had loved in many ways. As a friend, as a crush.

But the man before her? He stole thoughts from her head and sent her heart tripping all over itself.

"I'm sorry." It wasn't enough, but it was all she could say. Abigail twisted her cold fingers in her lap, trying to gather herself enough to afford Evan the same courtesy he'd offered her. "This thing with my dad—it has my head messed up."

He remained quiet. Waiting. Abigail dug deeper, pulling up more vulnerability from murky depths. "You have changed. So have I. We aren't the people we were a year ago."

They remained silent for a few moments while

people on the street scuttled by and cut them disapproving glances. Abigail didn't care what they thought about a man in the stocks and a tearful woman by his side. The reason they were stuck here in the first place surfaced, and she touched her chapped lips.

Evan had kissed her—opened up feelings she'd thought died a long time ago. Did she dare take a risk with him to see what could bloom between them?

She wanted to. Longed to. Still, terror engulfed her—the fear of the pain that could consume her if the relationship failed. How could she take that leap into the unknown?

Well, she'd fallen headfirst into the unknown of her current situation, and that hadn't turned out all that bad. Without this adventure, she might have never known Evan could love her. Or discovered the true depths of her own affection for him. She might not have seen firsthand the man he had become.

She would have never chosen this as her miracle, but now…maybe finding out what happened with her parents and their past wasn't all that important anymore. Maybe what mattered was discovering what she wanted for her own future.

Determination swelled. "I don't want to let their mistakes ruin my happiness." She hadn't really meant to speak out loud, but the admission brought Evan's head up.

His gaze slammed into hers. "And I don't want to

bear the consequences of another man's dishonesty."

Ouch. He had a point. She could only nod.

"Will you forgive me for what I said about you that night?" Evan asked, his tone serious.

Agreement formed on the end of her tongue, but his next words stole it away.

"Will you also forgive your parents for their choices and recognize you aren't doomed to repeat their mistakes?"

Oh boy. That's what she'd been doing, wasn't it? Sabotaging her chance with Evan because she feared she'd be deceived like her mother.

Could she forgive her father? A man who had lied to her for a lifetime and then, when she'd discovered the truth, kicked her out of his life? She couldn't. Not yet.

"Your bitterness won't change anything. It will only hurt you."

When had Evan become so philosophical? More disconcerting, how did he know her so well? She hadn't said a word, and yet he continued the conversation as though he'd read every thought that entered her head.

Cold wind tugged at her hair, skittering over her neck, and she shivered. Poor Evan must be freezing. She really should find something to cover him. Keep him warm. Maybe she could go find a jacket or—

She was avoiding again. Abigail shook her head against her own thoughts. Tentatively, she reached out and brushed the hair from his forehead. "I'm not ready to forgive my father yet. But I haven't been fair to you. All these feelings are a bit overwhelming." She tried for an ironic laugh, but the sound came out more as a pitiful squeak.

Evan crooked his head so he could see her. She held his gaze, hoping all she felt showed in her eyes. "Truthfully, knowing you care for me...like that...opened up all the feelings for you that I thought I'd buried a long time ago." Heat bubbled from her center at the way his eyes darkened, chasing away all thoughts of the biting cold. "All those things you said, the way you kissed me, well, seemed a little too good to be true."

The intensity in his face softened, and one side of his mouth pulled up in his trademark half-grin. The one that made her heart do backflips. How deeply had her sixteen-year-old self longed to see him look at her like that?

She cupped the side of his face, scooted closer underneath him, and gently pressed her lips on his.

Heaven help him. Evan returned Abigail's kiss. Gently. Sweetly. Infusing promises he didn't know if he could keep but desperately wanted to. The woman had sure sent him through the wringer.

She suddenly pulled back with a laughing gasp. "Probably better quit kissing you on the street before we both end up in jail."

He laughed despite his current situation. "These Puritans would drop dead after ten minutes in our world."

"Agreed." She settled back against the post.

They laughed at people as they passed, making up stories about why anyone would ever choose such ridiculous outfits. It reminded him of when they'd been kids people-watching at the mall.

They'd talk about what her kiss meant, eventually. But he knew them both well enough to know that spending a little while laughing would help them get to a place to discuss more serious topics. So he commented on powdered wigs and tricorn hats until his aching back made him lower his head, the muscles in his neck screaming.

How long had he been in this thing? It was hard to tell.

After a while she said, "I was wrong, Evan. I want us to trust one another. You were honest with me, and I want to always be that way with you, too. I'm terrified of what will happen if things don't work out between us, but I won't let that keep me from trying. I won't let the past have any say over what I want for the future."

Indecision stirred in him. Keeping things to himself seemed simpler. She was right. What did the past matter? But at the same time, she'd shared her secrets, her hurts. He owed her the same. "There's something I need to tell you."

She tensed.

"Back in college, right before I blew my knee out—"

"You there!"

The shout drew both their heads up. One of the guards who'd placed him in the stocks approached. The man lumbered toward them with an air of confidence. His hard gaze landed on Abigail, and his eyes narrowed.

They probably had a thing about her sitting by him, too. Good thing he hadn't seen the kiss. Without another word, the man shooed Abigail from her perch and produced a set of keys.

He leaned close to Evan's ear. "Don't say that I blame you for risking your neck for a go at that one, but best you keep your sins behind doors, aye?"

Sins?

Evan clenched his teeth. No more public affection. At least not until they got home. He wouldn't even hold her hand. The gruff man released him and walked away without ceremony.

"That was weird." Abigail made a face at the man's retreating back.

Evan offered Abigail his arm, and she slipped her hand through the crook of his elbow. "Now what?"

She let out a long sigh. "I suppose we ask someone the proper rules of courtship around here."

Courtship? Evan chuckled. He'd meant about the missed meeting at the Liberty Tree or their plans for the day. Good to know where her mind was. "Is that what you call dating in this time?"

Abigail gave him a coy grin, but before he could come up with a witty statement she sobered. "What were you going to say before the guard came back?"

They walked slowly along the edge of the road, mostly ignoring the milling people, the pungent smells, and the low of animals.

Time to air out his dirty gym bag. "One of the guys on the team, a second string wide receiver named Jeff Walters, accused me of taking unethical gifts. Said I was sleeping with this girl Chelsea Scarborough, and her father—remember him? He owns that bank on Union—was passing me money under the table. Opened an entire investigation with the NCAA. For reasons I can't fathom, Chelsea agreed with Jeff even though her father adamantly denied the accusations." The words leaked out of Evan like pus from an infected wound.

"No one believed me even though I didn't have the first perk to show for it. They were all quick to assume I would sleep with Chelsea for her father's money and influence with the boosters. The investigation almost cost me my scholarship."

They had only been words, but those words had haunted him. Too many people had easily believed the lies. The fact that no one thought him above such accusations had forced him to take a hard look at his life choices.

Abigail remained quiet. Contemplating. His stomach twisted. His football career was long over. After the injury, he'd lost his scholarship anyway, his future forever changed. It didn't matter now what they'd said. But it did matter what Abigail believed.

"You had a full scholarship and no reason at all to be taking compensation from a booster your senior year. None of that makes any sense. Frankly, I think it's ridiculous they even entertained the idea."

A weight slid from him, leaving a pulsing surge of relief. But a thought pricked him and the relief waned. She didn't believe he'd taken money. She didn't say anything about Chelsea. "I never even dated her. All I did was give her a ride back to her dorm one night. She'd had too much to drink." He shook his head. "No one had any problem thinking I lied about everything."

Abigail clung tighter to his arm. "Did she ever date Jeff?"

"Uh, no idea." What did that have to do with anything?

Abigail shrugged. "People often seek revenge because they've been wounded. Maybe she wanted to date you and you rejected her. Or you hurt a friend of hers and she wanted to hurt you. Maybe she was with Jeff and they conspired to harm you to somehow better Jeff.

I can only speculate."

They neared the Green Dragon and Evan steered her toward the door. "I don't know. After my knee, I didn't care to find out her motives. It didn't matter anyway. Only my parents thought the best of me. Everyone else believed I'd done exactly as she said."

But then, why wouldn't they? He hadn't done anything with Chelsea, but he'd made more than his share of mistakes before her. Choices he would erase if he could.

I'm not that man anymore.

He reminded himself again that his past sins were washed clean. Unfortunately, the consequences remained. And one of those consequences would likely be an uncomfortable conversation with Abigail about his past girlfriends.

Abigail gave him a squeeze. "I would have believed you."

Would she? Or would she have believed the worst of him as she had the night she'd heard him call her crazy? Maybe it didn't matter now. They were different people. He couldn't move on if he clung to the past. More than anything, he wanted a fresh start. Preferably with Abigail at his side.

They entered the front door of the tavern and were immediately met with the staunch presence of the owner. He lifted a hand to halt their progress. Dressed in a crisp blue jacket, dainty white hose, and wearing a curled wig on his head, the shorter man could almost be called comical. If not for the stern look pulling down his features.

"I'm going to have to ask you to seek alternative accommodations," Mr. Warren stated flatly.

"Why?" Abigail asked. "Is there a problem?"

Mr. Warren's gaze remained on Evan, his eyes sharp. "I cannot condone such wanton behavior under my roof."

Wanton behavior? Had they already heard about the kiss and Evan's time in the stocks? "I'm sorry, what?"

The man's face colored, though from anger or embarrassment, Evan couldn't tell. He lowered his voice, though no one else shared the entry hall. "You will not commit adultery under my roof."

Abigail tensed beside him. "We did no such thing!"

Mr. Warren glared at Evan. "I suggest you keep your companion under control, sir. Kindly remove yourselves from the premises immediately."

Abigail stepped forward but Evan caught her. He moved slightly in front of her, squared his shoulders to accentuate his height, and tried to imitate the authoritative and formal way of speaking he'd heard these people use. "I took up guard in the lady's room to protect her and nothing more," Evan snarled. Maybe speaking in these people's own terms would get through to him. "Surely your staff noticed two different sleeping arrangements?"

Mr. Warren shook his head emphatically. "Sharing a room with a woman not your wife is grievously unacceptable. Please collect your belongings immediately."

Evan withheld a sigh. So much for acting like one of them. Arguing with the man would do no good and would probably only lead to more trouble. Without further comment, Evan tugged Abigail up the stairs. When they made it to her room, he left the door open.

"Seriously. They take things a little too far." Abigail huffed. "I'll talk to Mrs. Hugley. Maybe she'll help us." Despite her words, her tone sounded unsure.

Evan focused on the task at hand. "We don't have any suitcases."

Abigail frowned. "We're really leaving?"

"Better that than being arrested. I wouldn't put anything past these people. We'll be seen as repeat offenders." Spying the heavy quilts spread across the bed, Evan snatched one and folded it in half. "Put all your clothes in that."

Abigail looked like she would argue, but then sighed and started pulling dresses from the wardrobe. She laid them in a neat stack in the center of the quilt. While she arranged the garments, Evan strode to his room down the hall. In a matter of seconds he'd gathered his colonial costumes and returned with them tucked under his arm.

He placed his clothes on top of Abigail's and folded

the edges of the quilt to create a bundle. "I guess this will do."

"How do we pay for the rooms? And that quilt?"

"No idea. Did you find any money with your costumes?"

Abigail shook her head. He hadn't either. Would they be thrown in jail for skipping out on a bill? Seemed like everywhere he turned in this ridiculous time he was facing incarceration. Evan gathered the bundle of clothing. "We'll leave as requested. Unless he asks us to pay for something, I won't bring it up."

She looked as though she might disagree but then gave a small nod and gestured him ahead of her out the door. Evan maneuvered down the stairs with his awkward load. Mr. Warren still stood at the bottom, his expression unreadable.

Evan stalked past him without a word, Abigail tight on his heels. Thankfully, the man said nothing about payment.

Outside, the bitter wind blasted him.

"Now what?" Abigail asked, rubbing her arms.

Question of the day. How was he supposed to know? He hadn't exactly studied up on Colonial Boston before going to pick up Abigail from the airport. But she was looking at him with luminous eyes as though he had the answers.

What was he supposed to do? They'd missed lunch, they had no money to pay for a different room or supper, and they had roughly three hours before it would start to get dark. Then they'd really be in a bind.

Evan closed his eyes, fighting off the sinking feeling in his chest.

A little help, God?

Somewhere in the distance, a bell began to toll.

Twelve

*W*hy hadn't he thought of this before? Evan grabbed Abigail's hand and tugged her in the direction of the bell sounding out the hour.

"Where are we going?"

"The church will help us." He stopped short to keep them from running into a woman in a starched cap pushing a hand cart. "We'll follow the bell." As soon as the woman passed, he grabbed Abigail again and tugged her along beside him.

"What? No." Abigail shook her head vigorously. "That's the worst place we could go."

Which direction? Evan struggled to separate the sound of the bell from the braying donkeys, rumbling carriage wheels, and Abigail's complaining. That way. West.

He turned Abigail in that direction, ignoring her protests. If anyone would help lost people, it would be the pastor at a church. If not him, then certainly his wife. Pastors' wives were a special gift from God. All he needed to do was find the minister, tell him about—

Abigail's hand suddenly snatched from his. She stumbled. Yelped.

He turned to reach for her. "Abs!"

Evan lunged, but time seemed to snag and then jerk into slow motion. He grabbed air. Abigail lurched forward, her hands flailing. Evan thrust his arms out to catch her, dropping their quilt bundle in the dirt. His fingers brushed fabric. Grasped.

And missed.

Abigail's feet caught on the long hem of her dress and she fell face first into the street. She screeched, trying to scramble up and yelling something unintelligible. Evan finally got his hands under her elbows and tugged her to her feet.

"It's on me!"

"What's on you? Slow down." Evan tried to understand the torrent of words that flew from her mouth, but his brain only caught on one.

Then the smell hit him. Manure.

Uh-oh. He glanced down the front of her gray gown, smeared from throat to knees in a brown substance.

Abigail clenched her fists at her side. "Look what you did!"

What he did? Evan blinked. Had he caused her to trip? He scrubbed a hand down his face. "I'm sorry. I didn't—"

She burst into tears, and he instinctively pulled her into his arms.

He ran a hand down her back. Felt her tremble. "I'm so sorry."

With her face buried in his chest, he couldn't understand what she mumbled, but he kept running his hand down her back anyway. After a moment, she pushed away.

"Now look at you. You're as disgusting as I am." Her brow scrunched, and her lips pressed together in an adorable pucker.

Evan laughed.

Mistake. Abigail swatted at him. "You think this is funny?"

What else could he do but laugh? The past two days had been nothing but one disaster after another. "At least we're dressed to match."

Her face scrunched again, but then she let out a chuckle. "I guess."

Evan wrapped an arm around her shoulder. No one on the street seemed to notice them. What was with these people? They were hyper-observant if he kissed her, but no one cared if the two of them were covered in manure?

"No church," Abigail said firmly, crossing her arms in defiance.

"Why?" He gathered their bundle before a man in a red coat could step on the quilt and ruin what might be their only source of warmth if he couldn't get them to a church. Evan frowned at the man as he passed, but the guy didn't seem to care.

Her arms uncrossed, and her fists landed on her hips. He wasn't sure which was worse. Her crossed arms and puckered face or her hands on her hips coupled with that look of feral dismay. Evan pressed his lips together to keep from smiling. He doubted Abigail would appreciate him finding her stance amusing. He knew he shouldn't find their situation funny, but the humor struck him in a way he couldn't quite explain.

"Why?" Abigail gaped at him, and he had to clear his throat to cover a chuckle. She flung an arm out. "Have you already forgotten the stocks?"

What did that have to do with the church? "Uh, no, but—"

"The church made those laws, Evan. These are staunch Puritans with strict moral codes. You really think those people are going to help *us*?"

His humor dissolved. "Maybe you're right."

"Trust me, you don't ever want to look for church people to help you. All they'll do is listen to your problems so they can share them with their friends at your expense."

"Did someone do that to you?"

Abigail straightened her spine. "It doesn't matter. A church here is the last place we want to go." She shivered and looked around. "But we do have to go somewhere. I don't want to spend the night on the street."

The thought sobered him further. There was no humor in spending a night outside in this freezing weather. "We don't have any money, and no one is going to rent us two rooms for free."

Abigail made a move to smooth her dress but then scrunched her nose and tucked her hands behind her instead. "I'm open to suggestions."

An idea formed, though it soured his stomach. *Forgive me, Lord.* He shifted his feet uncomfortably. "We could pose as husband and wife and ask if we can work in exchange for our bed."

Abigail opened her mouth as if to protest but drew a long breath instead. "That might work. Whatever we have to say to get out of this horrible cold."

Though she agreed, her expression said she found the idea as disagreeable as he did. But they had to do something. Abigail's nose was red, her pale cheeks flushed. She really wasn't meant for a northern winter.

"I'm sorry for the lie."

Her eyes darted from her survey of her dress to his face. "What lie?"

"Saying you are my wife. It's dishonest."

She shrugged. "Necessary." She said the word with so much strain that Evan guessed she'd spoken a lie of her own. The irony of them being a fake married couple wasn't lost on him.

If there's another option, God, I'm all ears.

"Which way?"

Evan nearly shrugged, but since she seemed to be looking to him to take the lead, he adjusted the quilt under his arm and motioned them forward.

You could make it true.

The idea nearly stopped him in his tracks. Evan coughed on a sudden intake of breath. No. That was extreme.

"What?" Abigail eyed him from under lowered brows. "What's wrong?"

"Nothing." He couldn't ask Abigail to marry him out of the blue. She'd barely agreed to dating him. Besides, he didn't have a ring.

Got any other ideas?

Nothing came to him, so Evan motioned for them to continue walking. They passed various shops and several buildings that didn't have any signs to identify their purpose.

They wandered around for a time, looking for any place that resembled the Green Dragon. There wasn't exactly a hotel on every corner in this place. Evan asked for rooms at two establishments, but neither place had any vacancy.

By the time they exited the third tavern, a place called the King's Boot, the sun had dipped close to the rooftops, making the ice droplets clinging to the shingles glimmer like diamonds. The streets were beginning to empty as the day lengthened and people hurried to their own homes.

Up ahead a steeple rose to the sky, backed by the warm glow of the sun. The church. They could ask for help, or…

No.

Evan pushed the ridiculous thought aside. He could *not* ask Abigail to marry him on the spur of the moment. God couldn't be nudging him to do something that crazy.

They neared the church, each step causing Evan's heartbeat to increase in an erratic rhythm.

I'm being crazy. Right, God? There's no way You're saying…? No. That's insane. Isn't it?

"I don't see any taverns here," Abigail said, pulling Evan from spiraling thoughts that weren't exactly working out as prayers.

"Huh?"

Abigail's gaze snagged on the church, and she shot him a scathing look. "You're still stuck on the church thing? I thought we agreed to find a room."

The church loomed in front of them, small yet inviting. Made of warm brick at the bottom with a wooden steeple pointed to the heavens. Tall windows of leaded glass reflected the sunlight. The building seemed to tug at him, pulling with invisible strings.

"That's crazy," he blurted.

"What is? The tavern?" Abigail marched in front of

him, blocking his path. He tugged his gaze down from the backlit steeple to her narrowed eyes. "We agreed the church would be trouble."

He nodded, but his feet refused to move. His eyes remained glued to the church building, and his brain felt like he'd ingested six gallons of caffeine. His thoughts were running everywhere, but he couldn't escape the tug of the idea of marrying Abigail.

A sign, maybe? Something to tell him God really was in this absolutely ridiculous thought that had his heart gripped so tightly he could barely breathe.

The doors of the church suddenly opened, and a smiling couple emerged. Dressed in ordinary clothes for the time, they clung to one another with shining eyes as they descended the front steps. Behind them, two older couples followed, all four smiling as well.

"A wedding." Evan barely breathed the words. A wedding. Here. Now.

Abigail frowned. "What? Evan, have you lost your mind? I have no idea what you are talking—"

Evan pointed behind Abigail, and she turned. The older couples embraced the younger one. One of the older men, with curled white hair that Evan assumed to be a wig, waved a hand, and a carriage approached. The young couple, who didn't seem to be more than teens, entered with smiles and waves to the others. The carriage driver cracked a whip, and the vehicle bounced away.

"Evan!" Abigail lifted onto her toes in an attempt to regain his attention. "What's gotten into you?"

"Marry me?" The words escaped his lips before he could catch them, almost as though his tongue had a mind of its own.

Abigail blinked slowly and lowered to the flat of her feet. "What...what did you say?"

Behind her, another wigged man dressed in a long black robe exited the church. Seized by a compulsion he couldn't understand, Evan raised a hand and called out. "Excuse me!"

Whatever Abigail exclaimed, he didn't quite grasp, though he thought she'd spat the word *idiot*. Evan hurried to close the distance and caught the man at the bottom of the steps.

The man tilted his chin up to regard Evan with blue eyes. "Yes?"

"Did you just marry that young couple?"

He bobbed his head. "You know them?"

"Would you be willing to perform another?"

Behind him, Abigail gasped.

"That is, of course, if my love says yes." Evan turned to find Abigail's face stricken.

He couldn't stop now. The minister stared at him. Abigail looked as if she might faint. Nonetheless, Evan grabbed Abigail's hand and dropped to one knee.

"Abigail Martin, I have loved you since we were kids, even if I didn't know it. Losing you was the hardest thing I've ever endured. These circumstances might not be what I pictured. I thought we'd date awhile. Not have a day-long colonial courtship. I'd planned on having a ring and a fancy dinner or something when I asked you."

Her mouth hung open. He was totally botching this.

"You've thought about asking me to marry you?" She stared at him, her head tilted to one side. "I mean before today?"

"As soon as I found out you were coming home, all the feelings that came crashing back told me there was only one outcome. I couldn't let you go again. Dating, the ring, then a little chapel somewhere." A nervous chuckle bubbled out of his center. "I mean, I hoped you'd agree to all that, of course."

He knew how ridiculous he must look. Kneeling on the ground, covered in manure. A bundled quilt filled with costumes at his side while he tried to convince a woman who'd only recently started talking to him again to marry him.

He didn't care. All that mattered was the over-whelming sense of rightness at asking Abigail to be his wife.

"Evan. This is crazy. You don't have to do this just so you don't have to lie when we get a room. It's fine. We will just get two rooms. We can get two rooms." Her voice became more desperate with each word. "Come on. Get up. You don't have to do this."

Evan kept a tight grip on Abigail's hand as she tried to tug away. From the corner of his eye, he saw the minister shift. But Evan kept his focus riveted on Abigail.

"I love you. I want to spend my life with you. We've known each other for years. Why do we need to date?"

Her mouth worked. Her cheeks blazed. "You want me to marry you? Right now? In a dress covered with poop?" She nearly shrieked the last word.

Evan glanced at the minister, who appeared as uncomfortable as Evan. "Uh, well, does that matter?"

"Does it matter? Are you kidding me?"

Why was she pulling away? He tightened his grip. "Marry me. When we get home we can do the white dress. The guests. The reception. As big of a party as you want."

Abigail shook her head. "This isn't at all how I imagined being proposed to. Get up."

Something told him he had to fight for her in this moment or he'd lose the chance. "You don't have to marry me here and now. Just promise me that you will. When you're ready. Promise me you will marry me, and I promise I will love you with every breath in my lungs for the rest of my life."

She couldn't breathe. Couldn't think. Evan was proposing to her in the middle of the street, both of them covered in manure. And for what? Just so he didn't have to lie to an innkeeper about their marital status?

She shook her head again, but he refused to let go of her hand. Wouldn't stop looking at her with those eyes filled with love and so much hope that it made her ache.

"Marry me?" he asked again.

Beside him, the wigged minister waited, watching her intently. What must he think? Would he throw them in the stocks? Or worse? A hint of a smile curved the mouth of his otherwise solemn face. Maybe not.

Evan waited. Still on one knee, breath coming out in puffs of smoke. She moistened her lips. "You're serious, aren't you?"

"I am."

But hadn't he asked only because they needed to find rooms? "Why here? Why now?"

A flicker of mischief sparked in his gaze. "I felt an uncontrollable desire to seize the moment."

Only Evan would say something that stupid. She never in a million years would have thought he'd do something so monumental in such a...well, like this. Roses, music, production. That was Evan. Charm and causing the girls to swoon. Not kneeling in the dirt with no other audience than strangers.

Her heart squeezed, and she sighed. "Evan. You're overcome by our extenuating circumstances. You saw a couple get married. Right now you think this would be a good idea for the weird situation we're in. But a week from now? A year? You'll regret asking." Each word lanced at her, cut her heart. Still, they must be said.

"Don't you trust me?" His voice was laced with pain, and her heart twisted again. He was making it so hard to be the logical one. To be the realistic one. "Don't you believe I meant everything I told you? Believe that I love you and want to marry you no matter where—or when—we are?"

She did. Didn't she? He'd laid out his heart. Okay, so maybe he wouldn't have if they hadn't been pushed to extremes, but then, maybe…? Could pushing them both to their limits have been the point of this entire adventure? To get them to share their pasts and their hurts, to be honest with themselves and each other? Would they ever have had the tough conversations back home in the present?

The truth you find won't be the one you seek.

Truth? Truth was she'd always loved Evan. Had always wished he'd love her. He'd laid his heart bare and still she couldn't let herself trust that he meant what he'd said. Why? Because her father was a liar?

She shook her head. No. That man wouldn't ruin her life. Wouldn't steal her chance at happiness. She wouldn't let him.

Evan's eyes squeezed shut. He started to rise.

"Yes, Evan. I will marry you."

His eyes flew wide. "Really?"

Abigail laughed. "Yes, really, you nut."

Evan lurched to his feet and swept her into his arms, twirling her around. She squealed and laughed against him. When he put her down, she felt as though she'd run a hundred miles her heart was hammering so fast.

"Are you prepared to speak vows?"

They both turned to the minister, who looked rather amused.

Now? "Oh no. Not in this dress. Not like this."

The minister seemed unperturbed. "If you'd like to freshen up, I'm sure my wife will have no objections."

"What do you say, Abs?" Evan's eyes sparkled with joy.

An impromptu wedding in Colonial Boston in the freezing cold without their friends and family?

How could she say no?

Thirteen

She really was crazy. When Abigail woke up that morning, she'd had no idea this would be her wedding day. Two days ago she didn't have a prospect of a groom. She hadn't been on a date in months. Today's walk and Evan's stint in the stocks didn't really count. Now they were about to take the plunge?

The minister's house was a modest dwelling tucked behind the church. Smoke rose from the chimney, and a few chickens clucked in the yard. Mr. Elmore, the preacher, ushered them inside with a barrage of words Abigail didn't quite catch. Something about the last vestiges of the day and hopefully they had all they needed in order.

No sooner had they stepped through the door than the preacher's wife showered them with welcome. She patted her white hair and tied an apron around her middle, all the while babbling welcomes and promising them a good meal. Abigail missed half of what she said. She cast Evan a look before the woman ushered her down a narrow hallway. She suddenly felt like a seashell caught in a riptide.

"You may freshen up in here," Mrs. Elmore said, opening the door to a cozy little bedroom. "There's a washbasin by the window."

"Thanks." She stepped inside. A fire crackled in the hearth and radiated delicious warmth through her body.

"Mr. Blake will be along with your possessions shortly," Mrs. Elmore continued. "As soon as he finishes speaking to Mr. Elmore." With that pronouncement, she closed the door, leaving Abigail to ponder yet another seemingly impossible situation.

Maybe they were being too hasty. Why rush something this important? Sure, time-travel had a way of putting one's priorities in perspective, but they should probably at least *try* to have a ceremony with Evan's family and their friends in attendance.

A nasty thought curdled in her stomach.

Unless of course this was a sham wedding. A lie. Something Evan saw as part of an act or a different life that didn't actually count.

No. Evan was *not* like her father.

A knock sounded. She turned to the door, her hand hesitating on the knob. Maybe she should call this off.

The thought caused an immediate, sharp pain in her chest she couldn't ignore. Nope. She and Evan would take the plunge, and she'd trust he wouldn't leave her to fall alone. She drew a deep breath, fixed a smile on her lips, and opened the door.

Evan stood in the dim hallway with their blanket bundle in his arms. "I think we should wait," he blurted.

Wait? He'd changed his mind about the wedding already? Doubts flared like a mushroom cloud. She should have known. Why in the world did she ever let herself get caught up in—

"I want to see you in a white dress. Give you a wedding you deserve." Evan smiled tenderly. "As much as I want to marry you as soon as humanly possible, I also want to give you everything you've dreamed of. And I'd like my parents there to see us."

Then why in the world had he asked her to marry him today? Obviously, neither one of them were thinking straight. He was right. If they were going to get married, then they should do it the right way.

Abigail released a breath. "They *would* be upset if they missed seeing you at the altar, all dressed up in a tux." She roamed her gaze over him. Even in a stained shirt and jacket, he looked awfully handsome. Then again, Evan could look good wearing a chicken costume.

"And I, uh…" He leaned close and whispered, "Sharing a small cabin with a preacher isn't exactly how I pictured our wedding night." Evan's cheeks were a strange shade of red. From embarrassment or the cold?

Abigail couldn't help but smirk until realization kicked in. *Wedding night.* Why hadn't she thought of that?

They'd barely had a first kiss. They weren't ready for a wedding night.

She let out a breath. "Right. Yeah. Let's wait." A weird sense of relief mixed with disappointment swirled in her.

Maybe she didn't care how or when she married Evan after all, so long as she did. But a wedding at home would mean a marriage license. It would be legal. Who knew what certifications they would have here? Certainly not anything that would be recognized back home.

"So, now what?" She still wanted out of this smelly dress.

"I guess we tell the minster about our predicament."

Abigail cocked an eyebrow. "Looks like we ended up going to the church for help after all."

"That's not—" Evan began, then snapped his jaw shut. The little muscle in the side of his cheek jumped. He took a breath and started again. "I didn't propose to you to trick you into taking help from a church."

Is that what he thought she'd meant? So much for trying to be cute. She squeezed his arm. "I know."

His shoulders relaxed. "I want to marry you. More than anything. But you deserve a beautiful wedding. With your friends. Our family."

The tenderness in his voice made her feel like a wobbly-kneed teen all over again. "As long as I have you, none of that matters."

The affection that filled his face swelled her heart. "I love you, Abigail."

Why had she ever avoided this man? Why hadn't she tried harder for their relationship? From now on, she would. That was the third time he'd told her he loved her, and she wouldn't let her own feelings go unspoken again. "I love you too." She barked out a laugh. "I think I've loved you since the ninth grade. I just maybe didn't recognize the truth that there'd never be anyone else for me."

Evan winked. "Always knew you had a thing for me."

Abigail rolled her eyes and slapped his shoulder. "You're something, you know that? Talk about a knack for ruining the moment."

He burst out laughing. "But you still love me."

That she did. Would she ever have admitted those feelings, even to herself, if not for coming here? Now she couldn't imagine *not* spending her days loving Evan Blake. So why shouldn't they make the commitment? Sure, it would be unconventional, and it wouldn't hold up when they returned home. But when in Rome...

"We could do both, you know," she said, thinking aloud. "We could speak our vows now. Be married between us and before God. But then we could wait until we get home for a normal wedding and the, uh, you know. The wedding night."

Evan grinned. "Works for me. Then maybe we'll get

a PDA pass while we're in this time warp." He handed her the bundle. "I'll wait for you to get ready." He winked again and strode away, perfectly content to marry her on the fly.

The fact that she was about to enter a kind-of-but-not-exactly legal marriage twisted her stomach into knots. Had her mother felt this way? Known she wasn't really marrying Abigail's father but choosing to take what she could?

Would Evan honor this pretend marriage when they got home?

Stop it!

She'd trust him. They'd have a real wedding when they got home. And if they never made it back—her stomach twisted violently at the thought. Living here, stuck in this strange time forever? Bile rose in her throat.

Please, God, get us back home.

She swallowed hard. She'd trust him to honor their marriage when they got home. And if they didn't…She drew a calming breath. If they didn't, well then they would deal with the legalities another day. For now, making a promise to Evan for a future together felt right. A terrifying, enormous, and life-altering promise, but right all the same.

Something in her gut said that agreeing to trust him, putting her faith in him, might mean almost as much to Evan as her declaration of love.

Decision made, she set herself to prepping for the occasion.

She undid the bundle and selected the pretty gold dress with red flowers and a sage green bodice she'd worn when she'd first arrived. It had a square neckline trimmed with delicate lace and ruffles flowing from the elbow-length sleeves. Abigail laid it across the bed.

Thankfully, she had to remove only the top layer this time. She peeled off the smelly dress and dropped it by the fireplace, then washed her face, neck and hands with cold water poured from a porcelain pitcher into a matching basin.

The clean dress slid on like a long robe over the top of the matching skirt and fit nicely. The pleats at the sides drooped a bit without the padded hip contraption, but she didn't mind. She'd struggled enough with the shape of her legs to even want to fake wider hips.

She quickly buttoned the bows across the front, glad she didn't have to worry with any ties behind her back.

Too bad she didn't have any makeup. Or even a mirror. Her fingers worked through the tangles in her hair and flew through a quick French braid. She wound the length of the braid into a bun and secured it with a tie at the base of her neck.

She'd done the best she could. A clean gown and a hairdo done without a mirror would have to be the extent of her wedding day preparations.

Abigail emerged from the room with a fluttering stomach.

"You look beautiful," Evan announced as soon as she stepped into the common space that featured a dining table, a large hearth with a cookpot, and a few chairs positioned by the fire.

Dressed in a clean shirt with lace bunched at his throat, he stood regally in the center of the room. This man was about to be her husband? He looked every bit as swoon-worthy as a storybook prince.

Mr. Elmore smiled and stepped toward Abigail. "Shall we start?" With Evan's captivating presence, she'd completely missed the robed man standing next to him.

The pastor's wife stopped whatever she'd been doing at a squat table near the rear of the room and came to stand by Abigail, her brown eyes alight in her round face.

Abigail had expected they would traipse back out into the cold and to the church, but the minister opened his large Bible and scanned the passages. Were they going to perform the ceremony in the middle of his living room? Maybe she had the Puritan thing wrong. Or maybe this man in particular wasn't as stuffy as she'd expected.

"Have you published the banns, or do you possess a license?" Mr. Elmore said, not looking up from where he turned pages in the Bible spread open in his hand.

They did marriage licenses back in the day? Maybe this would be more legal than she thought. Abigail almost chuckled. When they got home they'd have more than two centuries of marriage under their belts. Wouldn't their friends love to see them celebrate their two hundred fiftieth anniversary? How weird was that?

"Don't you give us the license?" Evan asked, pulling Abigail out of her thoughts about an anniversary party that would stir up all kinds of questions.

The man frowned. "If you haven't yet received one in order to proceed with the vows, we can have one drafted. Do you have proof of her father's consent?"

Abigail almost snorted. Her father's consent. Like she needed his permission.

Abigail glanced to Mrs. Elmore, but the woman watched Evan expectantly. Obviously such an outrageous statement was nothing out of the ordinary here. Evan glanced at her, an expression of helplessness on his face. If he said she didn't have her father's permission, the man probably wouldn't marry them.

"What's publishing the banns?" Abigail asked when an awkward silence settled on the room. Maybe they'd missed something in translation.

The minister blinked at her and then spoke patiently, as one would to a child. "The banns must be read for three consecutive weeks at your parish of origin as well as your intended parish home. Parishioners must have the opportunity to speak objections."

When neither she nor Evan responded, he cleared his throat. "As you are aware, there are two options for you to wed in the church. One is to first obtain the license stating you are legally able to wed and there are no objections. The other is to have the banns read and wait for any objections before proceeding. I cannot marry you without those provisions."

What happened to just saying that "speak now or forever hold your peace" line in the ceremony? How many people objected to weddings in this time that they had to go through such lengths?

Abigail rubbed her temple. "Look, maybe this isn't a good idea after all."

The minister drew back as though she'd reached out and smacked him. "Is it no longer your intention to speak commitment?"

"No, sir," Evan said quickly. "I mean, yes. We intend to speak commitment." The words sounded awkward. He glanced to her for help, but she could only nod her agreement. Evan gave a lame shrug. "We just thought we could say our vows tonight. You know, with you marrying us."

The minster shook his head and closed the large Bible with a thump. "If you are looking for a hasty handfasting, perhaps you can try the blacksmith in the morning?"

Blacksmith? Why in the world would anyone be married by a blacksmith? And what was handfasting? Didn't exactly sound legit.

Mrs. Elmore now looked uncomfortable. She kept

her eyes down and her fingers tangled in the white apron tied around her middle. Did she think they needed a rushed wedding because…what? They'd found out Abigail was expecting in the middle of the street, and Evan proposed right then?

Abigail's cheeks heated.

"We'll wait for a proper wedding," Evan said, casting her a sympathetic smile as though he'd been thinking the same. "I'm sorry for the confusion."

Talk about a disaster. They were getting married. No. They would wait. Well, they were part-way getting married. Now…a blacksmith or nothing? The emotional rollercoaster of this engagement had her stomach contents sloshing.

"Do you know where I can get a ring?" Evan suddenly asked. "I want this engagement to be real."

Mr. Elmore's brows dipped and then suddenly lifted with a smile. "Ah! I believe I understand now. Do you mean it's your intention before God to enter into *spousal de futuro* with Miss Martin? Is that why you've come to me?"

Spousal de futuro? What did that mean? It sounded something like spouse of the future.

"A marriage contract to be consummated at a later date?" the man supplied.

Oh. Like an official engagement?

Evan broke into a grin. "Yes! That. Thank you."

Mr. Elmore looked monumentally relieved, though

Abigail couldn't explain why one set of paperwork or another mattered so much to him. He let out a breath and smiled. "I can have the paper drawn for you in the morning," he said, tucking the Bible under his arm. "For now, I believe you young people are in need of a good meal and a night's rest. Correct?" He arched a knowing eyebrow.

"That sounds great. Thanks." Evan smiled again. Any more grins, and he'd be like a clown ready to pop out of a tiny car. What was with him? Trying to cover his nerves or had the former football star become uncharacteristically giddy?

The men shook hands as though they'd completed some kind of business deal. This had to be the strangest day of her life. First they were engaged by spontaneous street proposal, then she was supposed to have some kind of Vegas-style shotgun wedding, and now they were signing a contract that said they were kind-of married but not really until they consummated it? And how exactly was the minister supposed to know *that*?

She didn't have time to ask, however, since Mrs. Elmore hooked a hand through the crook of Abigail's elbow and dragged her toward the small table in the back covered with baskets and clumps of dried herbs.

"While the men work out the details, you and I shall begin on the vittles."

If that meant supper, she was all in. They'd missed lunch and the bit of mush she'd eaten this morning had long since left her stomach rumbling. She cast a look at Evan, who shot her a conspirator's grin, then followed the woman's lead.

Looked like she'd be cooking her own engagement celebration dinner. What would be next? Sewing her own wedding gown?

She cast one more glance over her shoulder. Whatever came next, Evan was worth it.

Fourteen

He'd never thought he'd be bartering muscle to pay for a meal. The next day Evan found himself chopping wood to cover the cost of a chunk of overcooked meat, a handful of stewed vegetables, and a pallet on the floor. Not that he minded. The pastor and his wife had been kind to take them in, and once he finished stacking a pile of firewood near the rear door, he'd have his paperwork.

Not the diamond to seal their engagement Abigail should have, but he'd get that as soon as he could. For now, he hoped a piece of paper would bring her peace of mind. Prove he meant everything he'd said and that he was committed to her.

He balanced the next log and brought the axe down. It skittered to one side, splitting the wood unevenly. With a sigh, he tried again. Nothing like a little lumberjacking to make a guy feel inadequate. The task had probably taken him longer than it would have the minister, but Evan was getting the hang of it. Sort of.

He paused to roll his shoulders. He'd removed his jacket, and the crisp morning air tickled the back of his neck. Life was much different here. Slower, more primal in a way, yet still prim and proper. He hadn't dared to hug his new fiancée last night before bed.

His fiancée.

Would she still be his when they got home, or had she been caught up in the craziness of this alternate universe they'd found themselves in? Their romance had been so hasty. One day she'd been shooting daggers at him and telling him to go away—after nearly a year of not speaking to him—and now she had agreed to marry him.

Would they go back to the way things were once they got out of this strange place? Maybe fear and stress had caused her to cling to something familiar.

She'd said she loved him. He'd fight for that, no matter what it took. There'd been too much truth in her eyes not to.

The axe rose and fell, slicing cleanly through the next log. Getting better. Maybe he wouldn't be entirely useless here after all. The thought that he might have a lot of new skills to learn pressed on him. Despite making mental plans for the future he and Abigail would share back in the twenty-first century, the very real possibility remained that this would be their new home. What if they never returned to the present?

Could he learn the skills needed to survive in a place

like this? His father was an old-fashioned kind of man, intent on raising his son with what Dad considered the basic principles of manhood. Integrity, honesty, and dependability. A man, Dad had always said, stood up for those who needed help. He supported his family. And he sacrificed for the woman he loved.

Dad could never have dreamed that sacrifice might mean learning to live in the 1700s. As the log pile dwindled, Evan tried to figure out a way to get them home. With no ideas how the time-travel thing worked, he finally turned his anxious mind to what type of work he could find if they were stuck here for any length of time. The thought of not having any control over his future brought a stab of panic. Taking a breath, he hefted the axe and let it fall, willing his anxiety to release with the motion.

Trust.

God was still teaching him to trust. True, he had no control over whether they returned to the future. He couldn't time-warp. Even if he could find a way to get them home, he didn't have any control back there either. The only thing he could control was taking each day God gave him and doing the best he could. If his days had to be spent living in the past, then he'd trust God to provide a way for him to take care of Abigail.

A week ago, figuring out how to provide for a wife had been the last thing on his mind. Now the idea nearly consumed him. The responsibility made him feel as though he'd grown ten years in the span of a few days.

Strange how extreme circumstances could do that to a man. Looking back, though, he could also see how God had been preparing him this past year. Teaching him to take his Dad's principles to heart. Showing him what it meant to be someone who made and kept commitments.

Thank you, Lord, for this unconventional trip. For Abigail. I'd like for us to go home and ask that you provide a way. But if it's your will we stay, help me figure out how to live here.

"Evan, are you all right?" His head snapped up at the sound of Abigail's voice. "Are you hurt?"

"I'm fine." He propped the axe on his shoulder and smiled at his bride-to-be.

Abigail stood in the doorway of the preacher's house, rubbing her arms against the cold. Her cheeks were tinged pink, and her eyebrows dipped together in concern. "Why were you standing there so long staring at your hand? I thought you'd cut yourself."

Had he been staring at his hand? "I was just praying."

She blinked, surprised. "Oh. Do you do that a lot these days?"

"Yep."

"Huh. Okay, well, breakfast is ready if you want to try my biscuits." She grinned. "Made from scratch."

She looked so adorably proud of herself he couldn't help but chuckle. "Awesome."

He propped the axe next to the chopping block. "I'll be in as soon as I get these pieces stacked for Mr. Elmore."

Abigail stepped out and pulled the door closed behind her. She surprised him by gathering up a few pieces and balancing them awkwardly in her arms.

"Thanks," he said.

"I'm learning to be useful."

Maybe she'd reached the same conclusion he had. Would they be able to learn the skills necessary to survive here? Her graphic arts degree and his training to work in sports radio certainly wouldn't do them any good. Not even his current "in the meantime" job at a car dealership would translate to Revolutionary War–era New England.

They carried and stacked the wood, working quietly beside one another for a few minutes, their breath billows of white in the morning air.

"Evan, can I ask you something?"

"Anything."

Abigail stacked pieces of wood, her face tight with more concentration than the task warranted. "Why does God reward bad people?"

Whoa. Where did that come from? "What do you mean?"

"Seems like there are a lot of liars and cheats in this world, and they're the ones who have it all."

She must be thinking about her dad's successful

company, which had allowed him the money to perpetuate his double life. Evan took his time answering, saying a quick prayer for wisdom first. "It's easy to take advantage in this fallen world. Easy to take the shortcuts, to live by the world's motto of *get what's yours*. But the Bible says God is not mocked. A man reaps what he sows. Eventually, we all face judgment for our actions."

Abigail looked out over the pastor's small yard. A few chickens pecked at the ground, clucking as they searched for insects. "I've been mad at God."

The whispered words held both guilt and sadness, and Evan stepped over to tuck her against his side. "Been there."

She looked up at him, something like relief shining in her eyes. "Really?"

"I lost my scholarship. Blew my knee out, and all hopes of an NFL career were over. My entire life had been wrapped up in my identity as a football player." He placed a kiss on the top of her head. "I was furious that God took everything from me. Only now I see that maybe He had a different plan for me all along. I've matured, grown in my faith, and learned that who I am isn't defined by my position on the gridiron. My worth and identity are centered on who God made me to be. Peace came with learning that."

Abigail snuggled against him but remained quiet.

"Sometimes I wonder what life would be like if all

of that hadn't happened," he continued. "I think I probably wouldn't be standing here with you." He nuzzled her soft hair. "I'd take a life with you over anything else. So I guess God had a better plan all along." The depth at which he meant the words almost surprised him. Would the man he'd been two years ago have thought so?

She trembled. Was she crying? He turned and cupped her chin, turning her face up to look at him. Two wet streaks glistened on her cheeks. "God's big enough to handle your anger and your questions. I'm here for you as you work through those. He has a plan in everything, and He can take what was bad and turn it into something good."

"Who are you?" Abigail said with a small laugh. "And what happened to that cocky running back I used to know?"

"You want him back?"

Abigail wrapped her arm around his waist. "I think I'll keep this version." They stood there a moment, and then she said, "I'll think about what you said. Thanks."

Before he could respond, she pulled away from him and grabbed the doorknob. "Now, let's eat before I freeze to death out here."

Later that afternoon they said their good-byes to the generous older couple and left the pastor's cozy cabin. Standing out in front of the chapel again, Abigail was beginning to worry that they would spend the rest of their lives wandering around Boston in the cold. At least the long woolen cloak and gloves the pastor's wife had given her shielded her from the nipping wind. She pulled the fabric tighter around her, thankful for the woman's kindness.

Bright sunshine bathed the city in a glimmering light that made the frost on the rooftops sparkle. The beauty almost caused her to forget the stench. But not quite. It would take more than a little glitter to cover up the filth of this place.

This morning she'd had to wash the manure from her dress. By hand.

The gown was still damp, bundled in the quilt Evan had slung over his shoulder. She opened her mouth to ask *now what?*, but the question had been so overused that she refused to ask again.

As though sensing her thought, Evan sighed. "I feel like we keep wandering around in circles. Pointless circles."

He was right. They needed a plan. "Any ideas?"

"Only one that I think could be of any use. Today is the sixteenth, right?"

"I think so. Why?"

"Tea party day."

Oh yeah. How had she forgotten? In the midst of everything else, the Sons of Liberty and their display had slipped her mind. "You think that's how we'll get home?"

"Weird as it sounds, yes. Remember that painting in the hallway back at the B&B?" Evan ran a hand through his hair, mussing his brown locks.

The one he'd been studying at The Depot. "Yeah. You were talking about it right before you blacked out."

"I'm pretty sure I saw myself in that painting. So I'm thinking that if I stand in the same spot here, maybe…" He shrugged.

"Maybe we can trigger the time warp," Abigail finished. "Worth a shot. Though I still don't know what information we were supposed to learn, or how that knowledge is going to send us home."

He tilted his head, eyes sparkling almost as much as the roof of the church. "I think we were supposed to learn we're meant to be together."

Her heart skipped. Had she ended up with exactly the same miracle as Maddie after all? Something she hadn't even known her heart longed for? She squeezed Evan's hand. "The answer we found wasn't what we were looking for," she mused. "I was looking for the truth about my father. Instead I found the truth about you. And me."

"Is it the miracle you wanted?" There was hesitation in his voice, as though he still wasn't sure about her feelings for him.

"No." The lines in his face tightened, and she brushed a gloved finger down his cheek. He'd nicked himself shaving with a straight blade this morning. She lifted herself on her toes to better meet his gaze. "But you were right. God had a better plan."

Evan leaned closer. She gave his face a little pat and lowered to the flat of her feet. "I'd *really* like to kiss you right now, but I'm guessing doing so out in front of the church will get us in a lot of trouble."

Evan chuckled. "Probably. Though this time I have paperwork proving we are—what did he call it?—future spouses."

She laughed and tugged his arm. "Come on. Let's go scout out the location you saw in the painting. See if that's our ticket home."

Home. Back to Ocean Springs and Evan's family. Had she really been worried about spending Thanksgiving with them? Now, she'd gladly share a room with Evan's older sister. Tight confines of a family staying together for the holidays? Awkward conversations and shared laughter? A sense of belonging?

Nothing sounded better.

Her father had given her a nice apartment, a car, and her dream job designing artwork for his advertising firm. But she'd been alone. All those things hadn't filled her heart. The more she'd tried to fill the hole, the larger it had grown.

She'd missed family. Evan's family. His mother. When her own mother had been angry with Abigail, had withdrawn her affections, Miss Connie had always been a steady presence. The loving woman Abigail had always thought a mother should be.

An ache bloomed in her chest. Mom had called Abigail crazy for her suspicions about her dad, but it turned out she'd been right all along. Had Mom secretly known and become angry with Abigail because she feared that truth getting out?

If they'd been able to talk through those feelings and find the truth together, would they have had a better relationship? The car wreck had stolen any chance of Abigail ever finding out.

Not being honest had cost her family so much.

Abigail snuggled against Evan's side as they slowly walked down the street, avoiding all puddles and piles. No matter how painful, she vowed to herself that from now on she would face her problems head-on, express her feelings, and be completely honest with those she loved.

She owed them—and herself—the chance for healthy relationships. She didn't want to repeat the disastrous cycles of avoidance and anger that had cost her a relationship with her mother—and had nearly caused her to lose Evan.

"What about a Christmas wedding?" Evan asked, drawing her from her thoughts.

Abigail almost asked why so soon, but yesterday she'd been ready to marry him in the middle of a stranger's living room. "Sounds beautiful. I can't think of any decorations prettier than white lights and poinsettias."

They planned as they walked, following the sounds of gulls toward the ocean. They'd have a small ceremony with friends and family under an arbor of sparkling lights at Evan's parents' house, and then they'd all go inside for dinner together. Simple, cozy, and utterly perfect.

"There they are!" Evan pointed to a cove that made up Boston Harbor.

Massive wooden ships floated in the water, their three spires topped with sails and rigging pointing to the bright blue sky. Canvas sails had been pulled tight, hanging like gathered curtains high in the air. The huge vessels bobbed up and down in the water, and as they drew closer, Abigail could see men scurrying around on the decks.

They continued up to a long wooden dock, then stopped to assess their location. Men darted around, all seeming to be in a great hurry.

"Is this the right spot?" Abigail hadn't really looked at the painting, and with so much commotion, it was hard to tell which one of the several piers would be their way home.

Evan scanned the docks. A head taller than everyone else, he had no problem seeing over the crowd that milled around. Men shouted to one another, and twice Abigail had to press into Evan's side to keep someone with an armload of cargo from bumping into her.

"Not sure," he finally replied.

Great. If Evan couldn't figure out where they were supposed to stand, then how were they going to trigger the wormhole?

"Maybe that building. Over there." Evan pointed to a large brick structure that squatted almost directly at the edge of the water. Square and covered with windows, it looked like some kind of office building. Strange. She wouldn't have expected an office complex. But then, they did conduct world trade in these times, or she and Evan wouldn't be here looking at ships loaded with British tea.

"I forget the angle," Evan said, pulling her out of her weird train of thought. "I remember seeing me, standing on a dock. There were big ships in the background. I was pointing at something…" His face scrunched in concentration.

A sense of anticipation tingled in her veins, but she couldn't be sure if the sensation came from the people around her or from within. There was a feeling of energy crackling in the atmosphere. It pulsed through the quick movements of men rolling barrels and carrying crates. The air seemed alive with nervous energy. As though the harbor knew that in a few short hours, history would unfold on this very spot.

"Down there!" Evan exclaimed. "That's it. I was standing right there." He pointed to the next pier.

Abigail gathered the side of her skirt to keep from being stepped on by a greasy looking sailor. She frowned at him, and he shot her a grin showing that half of his yellowed teeth were missing. She stuck close to Evan's side as he plowed through the crowd, not seeming to notice how people darted out of his path.

They elbowed their way onto the next long pier and stopped. Several smaller boats were tied to the posts on the dock, and men jumped in and out of them as they carried cargo to and from the larger ships out in deeper water. None of them seemed bothered by the cold or unsteady tide.

Evan released his grip on Abigail's arm and turned a small circle. "Yes. Here. I was standing like this…" He positioned his feet in a wide stance, shoulder-width apart.

Two dirty men hurried past him, one carrying a bundle while the other balanced a crate so large Abigail couldn't even see his face. She stepped aside so they could pass and peered down into the choppy water.

"I was pointing at something," Evan said behind her. "Like this."

She turned to look at him standing like a statue, pointing at one of the boats. He frowned, repositioned his feet, and pointed again. Abigail watched for ripples in the air or for him to collapse, but nothing happened. After a moment his shoulders sagged.

"I really thought this would do it."

Abigail looked back to the big ships. "Maybe we have to wait for the tea party to start. That's what was happening in the painting, right?"

A look of relief crossed his features. "Right. Of course you're right."

A rowboat bumped up against the side of the dock with a cluster of men and several large barrels on board. One short fellow in a flapping coat jumped out and secured the vessel with a thick rope. The others began maneuvering the barrels. Evan moved away as the first barrel hit the dock with thump.

"Guess we better find somewhere to hang out until the time comes," Evan said as one of the men rolled the barrel down the planks, narrowly missing his foot.

She turned to look back toward the town. Maybe they could find another inn or a restaurant with a dining room and a big fireplace where they could wait. "Preferably someplace warm. I wonder if they have hot choco—"

Something slammed into her back, knocking the rest of the words from her lips. She stumbled forward, arms flailing.

Behind her, shouts erupted. Abigail twisted, trying to right herself. Her momentum carried her toward the edge of the planks.

She screamed.

Then plunged headfirst off the dock.

Fifteen

old hit Abigail's body like a shockwave. She almost gasped, but managed to keep her lips sealed. The water wrapped tight fingers around her, pulling and tugging her to the murky depths. She sank deeper, the weight of her dress and cloak pulling her like an anchor. She struggled, desperately kicking her legs.

Panic wrapped deathly fingers around her stomach, urging her to fight on. But the water was too strong. The weight too heavy. Her muscles screamed.

Please, God. Help.

Her lungs burned, her body aching for air. She thrashed, no longer knowing which direction was up. Vision dimming, she willed herself to hold on.

Without her consent, her body convulsed. Her lungs sucked for air but found only icy water.

Pain seared thorough her chest. She heaved.

Choking.

Drowning.

Abigail bolted upright, coughing. Sweet, clean air

filled her nostrils, and she gulped it greedily. Her vision swam. Eyes squeezed tight, she panted for air as though she'd been holding her breath for ages.

She shivered against the memory of cold water. Of sinking.

What in the world?

Eyes searching, Abigail struggled to find reality. Her head pounded. Her lungs burned. She'd fallen. Went into the water. Drowned in the—

No. She was lying in bed, sheets soaked in sweat.

How did she get—?

Memories crashed through the fog and sailed on the rapid beat of her pulse, pounding through her brain in a jolt.

The time travel. Boston.

Evan.

She'd returned home. Or at least, to the inn in Ocean Springs.

Bolting out of bed, she ran out into the hallway of The Depot. "Evan!"

The hallway stood empty. Where did he go? Had he come back yet? She shouted his name again. Maybe he'd wake up in a different room. Like when they'd woken up at the Green Dragon. Yes. That had to be it. He was here.

Somewhere.

She shouted for him again, ignoring the feeling in her stomach that warned he wasn't here. That she'd gone crazy after all and had lived the last few days inside her own brain.

No. She knew what was real. She knew. And she would find him. Abigail jogged to one end of the hall, barely noticing the pajama pants she now wore instead of a long colonial nightgown. She banged on the first door, then the next and two more, not waiting for anyone to answer before hurrying to the next.

"Evan!"

Doors opened along the hallway, and sleepy people stuck their heads out. Old people, younger ones. Men. Women. None of them Evan.

Abigail addressed an older woman staring at her from a partly opened door across the hall. "Have you seen him? Tall, dark hair?"

The woman shook gray curls, her eyes wide in her face. "I'm sorry."

"Abigail, are you all right?"

She turned to find Mrs. Easley carrying a stack of towels. The other guests continued to stand in their doorways, staring.

"Where is he? Did he come back with me?" She grabbed the woman's arm, and the towels teetered. "Is he okay?"

Mrs. Easley smiled calmly at her. "Did you have a bad dream, dear?"

Dream? No way had all of that been a dream. She'd gone to the past. Got engaged to Evan. She—

"Let's go to your room and talk, shall we?" Mrs. Easley smiled sweetly again.

Abigail ground her teeth and called out to the on-lookers. "Did any of you people time-travel?"

A man with a trimmed beard, the elderly woman, and a middle-aged couple all stared at her from their doorways. Only the elderly woman looked at her with sympathy. The others seemed to think she was crazy.

She wasn't. She'd been there.

The painting! Of course. How could she have forgotten? Maybe she could activate it from this side. She darted around the innkeeper and down the hall to the painting of the Boston Tea Party.

Where was Evan? She squinted at the painted figures standing on the docks, but none resembled him. No figure stood pointing at the ships. No tall man with wide shoulders and a flashing grin. Tears blurred her vison, but she reached forward to graze the paint.

Would the painting send her back to him or bring him here? Either way, it didn't matter. So long as they were together. Her fingertips brushed the canvas. She waited for a tingle. A burst of light.

Nothing.

No!

She grabbed the frame and shook it but remained utterly alone. Her throat clogged.

Mrs. Easley wrapped a comforting arm around Abigail's shoulder and leaned close to her ear. "Everything will be all right, dear. Come with me. Let's talk."

Abigail allowed Mrs. Easley to guide her back into her room. Her suitcase sat open on a stand, her clothes neatly folded inside. The tall four-poster bed had been slept in.

But it wasn't a dream. It wasn't!

Mrs. Easley closed the door softly behind her.

"What did you do?" Abigail demanded. She clenched her fists at her sides. "I know I'm not crazy. I know you sent me to the past."

Mrs. Easley remained unnervingly serene. "Such things are quite beyond my ability, I assure you."

"But you wrote the letter. I know you did. You opened the door in that costume, and we went to 1773. I fell in the water. Where is Evan?" The words burst out of her in blasts of panic. She had to find him. Had to. She couldn't lose him again.

Had he stayed in the past? What if she never saw him again?

She glared at Mrs. Easley. "Where is he?"

"I don't know." She spoke softly, her eyes filled with compassion. "I'm only the stationmaster, you see, not the Conductor."

What? What kind of nonsense was that? "Are you actually saying you didn't send me back to the past? That I dreamed all of it?" She stepped closer, panic causing her throat to burn. "Please. Tell me the truth. What happened?"

Mrs. Easley closed her eyes for a second, then offered a small smile. "Reality is a bit more…fluid than we might imagine, don't you think? Does it matter if you went physically to another time and place or if you saw everything in a dream?"

"Of course it matters. One is real. The other is made up."

Mrs. Easley nodded thoughtfully. "Tell me, did you live those days? Experience trials and emotions?"

"Yes." So many emotions. Experiences she couldn't have made up in her head. Evan's love for her. She *needed* that to be real.

"Do you remember everything you learned?"

Her breath caught. "I remember everything. I lived it. I know I did."

"Then that is the truth you experienced. What does it matter how it occurred?"

Abigail shook her head. She couldn't accept that everything had been a dream. Those days had been too vivid. Too real. "What about Evan? He was there. I didn't make that up, did I?" She hadn't made up his feelings for her.

Had she?

"Mr. Blake was very much a part of your journey," Mrs. Easley said, sounding resolute. "Did he teach you anything?"

That he loved her. That he had matured into a strong, honorable man. Someone she could trust with her life. Her heart. But she sensed that wasn't the answer this woman sought. She nodded slowly. "He said sometimes God has a different plan than the one we expect. He believed that those plans were even better than our own."

"Do *you* believe that?"

Did she? Abigail sank on the bed. If everything had been a dream, then could she trust what she learned there? She pressed her lips together in concentration. Mrs. Easley seemed content to wait while Abigail sorted through her thoughts. Whether or not the experience itself had been real, the way she felt was.

Somewhere along the way she'd let down her protective walls. Had realized she wanted to let go of her bitterness, her pain. She wanted to build a new future. With Evan.

Maybe he hadn't been there. Maybe he'd never declared his love for her. But her love for him was real. Abigail stood up straight.

"I love him."

Mrs. Easley smiled.

She loved him, and he needed to know. Dream or not, the experience had given her truths. Truths she would now have to work out. She needed to trust the goodness of God. Somehow she'd have to learn how to forgive her father.

But right now, she had to tell Evan she loved him.

"You'll be checking out now, I take it?" Mrs. Easley

asked, her warm eyes sparkling.

Abigail nodded. She had something she needed to do.

His head hurt like he'd split it open. Evan groaned and rolled to his side. Had he lost control of the preacher's axe and dropped it on his skull? No. He'd finished that chore.

Went down to the docks. Hadn't he?

Evan forced his crusty eyes open and stared at the ceiling fan. He frowned, trying to think through the fog. Something was wrong.

Memories came flooding back. Boston. The ships.

Abigail.

She'd fallen into the water. He bolted upright and untangled himself from the sheets. Where was he? He stood on a carpeted floor, every muscle tense. His body ready to launch at any threat.

High school football trophies. Band posters. His breathing slowed. He was in his old room at his parents' house?

But how? He'd gone to the airport. Had gotten Abigail. Went to that weird B&B. They'd…they'd gone to the past. She'd fallen into the water.

He'd jumped in to save her. Had felt the panic of

losing her in the depths. And then…nothing.

A dream?

Evan turned slowly around the room. His suitcase sat on the floor in the corner, contents rifled through. Dirty clothes littered the floor. He wore pajama pants and an old MSU football shirt.

All of it had been nothing but a dream? Impossible. He'd never had a dream that real in his entire life. How had he gotten here?

He rubbed his temples. He had to get back over to that creepy old Victorian house. Find Abigail.

A knock sounded at his door. "Evan?"

Sarah. He opened the door to find his sister holding a mug of coffee. She smiled at him. "What time did *you* get in last night?" Her blue eyes sparkled with mischief.

"What?"

"I went to bed at midnight and you still weren't back from dropping Abigail off." She exaggerated wiggling her eyebrows. "Did you tell her how you feel about her?"

Evan gave her a flat look. "Shouldn't you be a bit more professional?"

She sobered. "Are you all right? Did something happen?"

Evan rubbed his temples. "I don't remember. I took Abs to the inn. I blacked out. Next thing I remember, I'm here." Minus, of course, the entire Colonial Boston part.

Sarah frowned. She stepped closer, her keen eyes sweeping over him. He could trust her. She wouldn't think he was crazy. Not entirely.

"I had this…dream. I guess it was a dream. I went to Boston for the Boston Tea Party. Well, we never made it to the actual tea-dumping part." He shook his head. "It felt so real. I lived there for days, Sarah. We slept and woke up again. They put me in the stocks. Abigail fell into the water, and I jumped in to save her. She was sinking. And then, I was here."

Sarah studied him. Did she think he'd lost his mind? She was the shrink. She would know. His insides tightened. Maybe he *had* lost his mind. Been stressed over seeing Abigail again and made up a situation where he could tell her how he felt and—

Suddenly Sarah sighed and rolled her eyes. "Ha. Ha. Very funny. Will you ever grow up?" Laughing, she turned and walked down the hallway. "Better get dressed," she called over her shoulder. "Mom is sending you to Kroger."

Day-before-Thanksgiving grocery shopping? Old ladies with carts were as ruthless as an LSU defensive line. Worse, maybe.

Evan closed the door and sat on the bed, trying to come to grips with what had happened. What were the facts? Sarah knew he'd gone to pick up Abigail and take her to the B&B. Obviously he'd come to his parents' house that same night.

Days hadn't passed while he'd been in Boston. He hadn't even woken up on the floor at the inn. So that left only one logical conclusion.

A dream.

But it had been so real. He'd told Abigail how he felt. She'd loved him back. They'd been engaged. Planned a Christmas wedding.

All of that had been in his head?

He set his teeth. Maybe. Maybe not. One thing he knew for certain.

It was time to tell Abigail he loved her. Maybe the dream had been showing him that. A vision, maybe. Showing him that, if they worked through some things, they could be together. That if he was patient and persistent, he could win Abigail's heart.

Dating her wouldn't be enough. His heart still held the warmth that had come when she'd accepted his spontaneous proposal. Dream or not, he wanted that feeling again. Maybe it had been a sign showing him what he needed to do.

Decision made, Evan rushed to get dressed. Kroger would have to wait. Mom would understand. He was going after Abigail.

But first, he was going to get a ring.

Sixteen

She'd lost her mind. Abigail was sure of it this time. She thanked the rideshare driver and stepped out into the salty crisp air of an Ocean Springs November. Her stomach tightened.

I can do this.

Her feet wouldn't move. Wouldn't take her closer to Evan's parents' house. To the truth she had to share. Tucked into a quiet cul-de-sac, the Blakes' house boasted painted pumpkins on the wide front porch and ribbons wrapped around the white posts in autumn browns and reds.

Abigail stood on the sidewalk, suddenly remembering being an awkward girl from two streets over. They'd been neighborhood kids together. It seemed like a lifetime ago.

She'd spent the entire ride over here praying, but she still didn't feel prepared.

Running from God had been foolish. Like swimming away from the lifeguard who was trying to keep her from drowning. She'd asked for forgiveness. Knew she had to extend a little of her own.

But first, she needed to be honest with Evan. She'd already forgiven him for what happened the night before she'd left. Now she needed to ask his forgiveness for shunning him. The tough conversations they'd had in Boston—well, she'd have to go through all that again.

Evan was worth it. Maybe he loved her. Maybe he didn't. But she owed herself—and him—the chance to find out. Gathering her courage, Abigail strode toward the door, her suitcase rattling behind her.

The doorbell chimed merrily inside, and a few moments later Evan's mother opened the door.

She grinned, causing two dimples in her round cheeks. "Abigail! You decided to come after all." She grabbed Abigail and pulled her into a tight embrace. "We've missed you."

No condemnation. No angry words. Only acceptance and love. Tears stung Abigail's eyes. She returned the older woman's embrace, feeling her heart swell. "I missed you too, Miss Connie. I'm so sorry I left without saying good-bye. I should have…" Her voice hitched. "You deserved better. I'm so sorry."

"Hush now. It's all right." Miss Connie stroked her shoulder and pulled back to arm's length. "We know you went through a lot. Losing your mother and all. I just wish you'd known we were here to help you." She gave Abigail a squeeze. "Still are."

Tears escaped and ran down her cheeks. "Thank you."

"I'm so glad you decided to accept Evan's invitation." She glanced to the porch. "Oh, good. You brought your suitcase. You'll stay with Sarah in her old room. She'll be so excited to see you again. You always were a little sister to her."

Miss Connie prattled on as she gathered Abigail's luggage and shooed her inside. A sense of welcoming and warmth enveloped her.

Thank you, Lord. Even if all of that trip was nothing more than a dream, thank you for using it to teach me. To show me your mercy and grace. To make me realize how much I love Evan and his family.

Before she could ask, Miss Connie said, "Sarah came in yesterday. John had to go into the office this morning, but he should be home for supper. Probably just pasta for tonight, seeing as how I've got enough to feed twenty tomorrow you know." She waved a hand as though nothing pleased her more than making way too much food for five people. "I sent Evan to the store to get a few things I forgot, but he should be back anytime now." She placed Abigail's suitcase at the bottom of the stairs.

Relief swelled through her. Evan wasn't stuck in the past. He had to have been here for Miss Connie to send him out on errands.

Yet a piece of her heart sank with the confirmation.

A dream after all. She'd held onto a shred of hope that they'd really gone back in time together. But if Evan had gone on a time-travel adventure with her, he would have been telling everyone. Coming after her. Not buying groceries. She withheld a groan.

So she had to start over back in reality. She could do that.

"Hey!" Sarah exclaimed, bounding down the stairs. "There you are. Got any news to share?" Sarah grinned in a conspiratorial kind of way.

Abigail's heart sputtered. Did she—? How would she—? "What?"

Sarah looked at her like she could see straight through Abigail's thoughts.

"I, uh…" Should she tell the psychologist that she'd thought she and Evan went back to the past? Had Evan already told her?

"You mean that doofus still didn't say anything?" She shook her head. "Classic avoidance syndrome," she muttered.

"Tell me what?"

Sarah gave her a sly look. "I'll let him do that. If he ever gets the guts. In any case, at least you accepted Mom's offer to stay with us." Tenderness softened her features. "We've really missed you."

"I missed y'all too."

An understanding passed between them, and Sarah said, "You know the good thing about new seasons? They offer new opportunities."

Abigail could only nod. New opportunities. Probably not a Christmas wedding, but the chance to tell Evan she loved him. He might not feel the same, but she would never know what might happen if she lived in fear. An old voice tried to tell her she would never be enough for Evan Blake, but she ignored the lies. In time, maybe the nagging would go away.

In the meantime, she'd just keep praying and asking God to walk with her each step of the way. No matter what strange journeys she went on.

"You two coming?" Miss Connie called from the kitchen. "I could use some help with these cookies."

Laughing, Abigail followed Sarah into the kitchen.

Half an hour later, she'd been tied up in a frilly apron, given hot cider, and had her hands knuckle deep in cookie dough. Miss Connie was sharing a story about Evan getting stuck in a tree when he was little.

"Poor boy thought that bird was crying out for help," Miss Connie laughed. "Thought he had to climb up there to rescue it. He was fuming mad when that thing flew off."

Abigail laughed, picturing an adorable seven-year-old Evan shaking his fist at a bird.

The front door slammed, and Miss Connie grinned. "That would be the rest of my ingredients." She dusted her hands on her apron. "In here!"

Footsteps pounded through the hallway, coming closer. Abigail's heart hammered. She could do this. Pretend the past few days hadn't happened while learning from them as though they had.

Evan appeared in the doorway. His eyes slammed into hers.

"I found you." The words escaped from his lips with awe. He'd been looking for her?

Did he…? She yearned to run to him. Throw herself into his arms. But his eyes held her rooted to the ground. Searching…knowing? Did he remember?

"Where are my groceries?" Miss Connie demanded. "Did you leave them in the car?"

Evan strode across the room, ignoring his mother. His gaze bore down into hers.

"I thought I'd lost you." He cupped her face. She leaned into him. The words were layered with meaning.

"Evan." She breathed his name. He pulled her against him. "I'm so sorry," she said into his chest. "I have so much to tell you." The thoughts in her head swirled. Did he know about Boston? Or had he only seen her feelings written all over her?

Did it matter?

Evan eased her back, his eyes searching her face. "Does it…?" He hesitated, then tilted his head. "Does what you have to tell me have anything to do with tea parties?"

Her breath caught. "You—" She sucked in air and tried again. "You know? It wasn't…it wasn't in my head?"

A grin split his face, and he let out a hearty laugh. "Guess it wasn't in my head either."

"What in the world are you two talking about?" Sarah asked.

They ignored her. Evan was here. He remembered. It couldn't have been a dream. Not one they'd both lived.

That meant they'd been there. Everything that happened had been real.

Evan pulled back, a smile playing on his lips. Lips she longed to kiss.

"I thought I'd have to retrace a few steps first, but since that doesn't seem to be the case, I'm not waiting any longer." He dropped to one knee.

Miss Connie squealed.

Sarah gasped.

Abigail could only stare at him.

He reached into his pocket and pulled out a black box. "Better than mud and manure, right?" He winked.

She laughed. "Definitely."

"This is the weirdest proposal I've ever heard," Sarah whispered.

Her mother shushed her.

Evan cleared his throat and shot his sister a warning look. He smiled up at Abigail. "I still don't have that fancy dinner. But this time I've got the ring."

"Looks like I'll be the one going to Kroger," Sarah mumbled.

"Will you hush!" Miss Connie barked. "You're ruining this."

Abigail laughed. They weren't ruining anything. Being here, with Evan and his family, she couldn't think of anything more perfect.

Evan glared at his sister, but Abigail took his face in her hands and turned him back to her. "Yes. No matter where or when, yes."

That grin she so loved split his face wide, and he fished the ring out of the box. A marquise cut diamond glittered on a silver band. Simple and elegant. Evan slid the ring on her finger.

"Perfect," he said. "Just like you."

Abigail threw her arms around his neck and pulled him close.

"See what you did?" Miss Connie grumbled to Sarah. "You got him so flustered he didn't even ask her. You messed up the whole flow."

But he had asked her. There in the street, dirty as they were. It had been *real*. Evan's love for her had been—and was—real. She leaned back and ran her fingers through his hair. "Are we still on for a Christmas wedding?"

Evan shrugged, though his eyes sparkled. "I guess I can wait that long. If you insist."

Abigail laughed again, then took his face in her hands. "I love you."

He grinned. "I know."

His lips found hers, and the rest of the world melted away.

Epilogue

Christmas Eve

$\mathcal{H}$e'd never seen anything more beautiful. Evan hardly noticed the decorations his mother and sister had spent the past two days constructing. He was sure the sparkling white lights on the arbor and the red poinsettias were nice and that the women had made sure Dad arranged the folding white chairs to perfection.

Somehow they had turned his parents' backyard into a glittering winter wonderland. Abigail had been thrilled.

But no decoration in the world could compare to the sparkling gem that was his bride.

Abigail slowly stepped forward from her place on his parents' back porch, her hand looped through his father's arm. Dad smiled at Abigail with affection as they took a step down the grassy aisle.

Long curls cascaded over her shoulders and lay against the white of her long-sleeved gown. Tiny white flowers nestled in a crown on her hair. Her luminous eyes sparkled at him.

Evan swallowed against the tightness in his throat. *His bride.* The woman who had always been his truest friend. The beauty who he still couldn't believe had accepted him—flaws and all.

Violin music played from a speaker somewhere behind where Sarah and Abigail's friend Maddie stood as bridesmaids, holding handfuls of red Christmas flowers. The night air was crisp enough to keep him from sweating through his coat and tie.

Finally, Abigail reached the front, her smile intoxicating.

His father patted her hand and joined Evan's mother in the first of two rows of chairs. His grandparents, aunts, uncles and cousins filled the rest. Abigail's father hadn't come. Nor would he return any of Abigail's calls. The hurt still burned in Abigail's heart, but Evan would be there to help her through it.

He'd love her with everything he had and point her to the One who healed all wounds.

Abigail took his hands in hers and smiled up at him. The preacher talked on about the sanctity of marriage and the commitment they were making to one another.

"You look amazing," Evan whispered.

"So do you," she whispered back. "This is everything I dreamed it would be."

Her words warmed him, and for a moment he lost himself in the magnetic pull of the love in her eyes.

The preacher cleared his throat. Evan glanced at him.

"Evan Blake, do you take this woman to be your wife?"

He did. To be his wife, his heart, his friend. Through the joys and trials of life. He'd cherish every moment with her. "I do."

They exchanged rings, and the vision across from him pledged to bind her life to his. He felt as jittery as a freshman at his first Egg Bowl. But rivalry games had nothing on the anticipation zipping through him now. A life with Abigail was the most exciting adventure he could imagine.

"I now pronounce you husband and wife," Pastor Miguel announced. He smiled at Evan. "You may kiss your bride."

Evan grabbed Abigail and pulled her to him, tipping her into a dramatic dip.

She laughed, cradled in his arms. "This is quite the display, Mr. Blake."

He winked. "That it is, Mrs. Blake. Good thing there's no one here to toss me in the stocks."

Amid the cheers of the people he loved the most, Evan kissed his wife. She grabbed his neck and pulled him closer, sealing the love that would be theirs to share for a lifetime.

No matter what new adventures their future held.

Books by Stephenia H. McGee

Ironwood Plantation
The Whistle Walk
Heir of Hope
Missing Mercy
*Ironwood Series Set
*Get the entire series at a discounted price

The Accidental Spy Series
*Previously published as The Liberator Series
An Accidental Spy
A Dangerous Performance
A Daring Pursuit
*Accidental Spy Series Set
*Get the entire series at a discounted price

Stand Alone Historical Titles
In His Eyes
Eternity Between Us

Contemporary
The Cedar Key

Time Travel

Her Place in Time

(Stand alone, but ties to Rosswood from The Accidental Spy Series)

The Hope of Christmas Past

(Stand alone, but ties to Belmont from In His Eyes)

Novellas

The Heart of Home

The Hope of Christmas Past

www.StepheniaMcGee.com
Sign up for my newsletter to be the first to see new
cover reveals and be notified of release dates
New newsletter subscribers receive a free book!
Get yours here
bookhip.com/QCZVKZ

About the Author

Award winning author of Christian historical novels, Stephenia H. McGee writes stories of faith, hope, and healing set in the Deep South. She's a homeschool mom of two boys, writer, dreamer, and husband spoiler. Stephenia lives in Mississippi with her sons, handsome hubby, and their fur babies.

Visit her website at www.StepheniaMcGee.com and be sure to sign up for the newsletter to get sneak peeks, behind the scenes fun, the occasional recipe, and special giveaways.

Facebook: Stephenia H. McGee,
Christian Fiction Author
Twitter: @StepheniaHMcGee
Instagram: stepheniahmcgee
Pinterest: Stephenia H. McGee

Made in the USA
Middletown, DE
15 March 2022

62625703R00142